D1084211

The Brotherhood
of the Grape

Also by John Fante

Novels
Wait Until Spring, Bandini
Ask the Dust
Full of Life
My Dog Stupid

Short Story Collection
Dago Red

Screenplays
Full of Life
Walk on the Wild Side *(in collaboration)*
Reluctant Saint
My Six Loves
Jeanne Eagels *(in collaboration)*
My Man and I
Something for a Lonely Man
Maya
Are These Our Children?

The Brotherhood of the Grape

A Novel by John Fante

Houghton Mifflin Company ᴅᴜᴄᴛᴇᴅ 1977

Library of Congress Cataloging in Publication Data
Fante, John, date
The brotherhood of the grape.
I. Title.
PZ3.F218Br [PS3511.A594] 813'.5'2 76-54684
ISBN: O-395-25046-3

Printed in the United States of America

V 10 9 8 7 6 5 4 3 2 1

For Joyce, of course

The brotherhood of the grape! You see them in every village, these old rascals, loafing outside the cafes, drinking wine and sighing after every passing skirt.

— Eduardo Verga, *The Abruzzi*

The Brotherhood
of the Grape

1

ONE NIGHT last September my brother phoned from San Elmo to report that Mama and Papa were again talking about divorce.

"So what else is new?"

"This time it's for real," Mario said.

Nicholas and Maria Molise had been married for fifty-one years, and though it had been a wretched relationship from the beginning, held together by the relentless Catholicism of my mother who punished her husband with exasperating tolerance of his selfishness and contempt, it now seemed utter madness for these old people to leave each other at such a late time in their lives, for my mother was seventy-four and my father two years older.

I asked Mario what the trouble was this time.

"Adultery. She caught him red-handed."

I laughed. "That old man? How can he commit adultery?"

In truth it was the first accusation of this type in many years, the previous one having to do with my father's forays upon Adele Horner, a postal employee — "a crooked little witch," my mother had described — a woman of fifty with a slight limp. But that was years ago, and Papa wasn't the man he used to be. Indeed, on his birthday in April I had seen him hunched on the floor, groaning and pounding the rug with both fists as he fought off an attack from his prostate gland.

"Come on, Mario," I chided. "You're talking about a burned-out old man."

He answered that Mama had discovered lipstick on Papa's underwear, and upon confronting him with this evidence (I could see her thrusting it under his nose), he had seized her by the neck and throttled her, bending her over the kitchen table and booting her in the buttocks. Though he had been barefoot, the kick had left a purple bruise on Mama's hip and there were red blotches at her throat.

Ashamed of the cowardly attack on his wife, my father fled the house as Mario entered the back door. The sight of Mama's abrasions so enraged him that he rushed outside, leaped into his truck, and sped off to the police station where he sought a complaint against his father, Nicholas Joseph Molise, charging him with assault and battery.

Chief Regan of the San Elmo police tried to dissuade Mario from such drastic action, for he was an old drinking crony of my father's and a fellow member of the Elks Club. But Mario pounded the desk and held to his demands, forcing the chief to do his duty. Accompanied by a deputy, Chief Regan drove to the Molise house on Pleasant Street.

To Mario's disgust, my old man refused to submit to arrest and stood his ground on the front porch, armed with a shovel. A crowd of neighbors quickly gathered and my father and the chief slipped into the house and sat at the kitchen table, drinking wine and discussing the situation while Mama wept piteously from the bedroom.

By now the crowd in front of the Molise residence had spread into the street and two extra police cars were summoned to cordon off the whole block. Suddenly the camaraderie between Papa and the chief came to an abrupt end. The chief produced handcuffs and hostilities broke out. Deputies rushed in when Regan yelled for help, and my father was pinned to the floor and shackled. Breathing heavily, he was dragged outside to a police car.

The sight of her spouse in irons drew cries of anguish from my mother. She rushed the police, swinging and clawing with such frenzy that she fainted on the sidewalk, where her neighbors, Mrs. Credenza and Mrs. Petropolos, dragged her, heels bumping, into the house.

My brother Mario, having reverted to his helpless fear of my father, now reappeared from behind the garbage cans in the alley and hurried to Mama's side as she lay on the couch, consoling her and holding her hand.

Trembling with a desire to forgive her husband, Mama rose haltingly, reeling across the room to drop to her knees before the statue of Saint Teresa, imploring the Little Flower not to punish her wayward spouse, to look with pity once more on his transgressions, and to plead before the court of Almighty God for his immortal soul.

She begged Mario to drop the charges against the old man and secure his release from the San Elmo jail. "He's old, Mario. He don't mean no harm, but he's losing his mind."

At first Mario refused to consider freeing his father, preferring that Papa remain in the slammer for a few hours to cool off. But my mother's lamentations, her noble forbearance, and her warning that Papa would tear his son to pieces unless quickly freed made Mario relent. She and Mario drove downtown to spring the old man.

"What else could I do?" Mario implored over the telephone. "He's a mean, vicious old man, and the longer you lock him up, the meaner he gets. He's a mad dog."

To their astonishment, and to the disgust of Chief Regan, Nick Molise did not wish to be released, nor would he hear of a dismissal of the charges. Cursing Mario and Mama, sneering at his captors, he freely accepted captivity, vowing to fight his case through every court in the land, even to the Supreme Court, to prove that there was still justice in America.

"Then he spit in my face," Mario said. "He said I was Judas who killed Christ. He said I wasn't his son anymore. And then he kicked me in the stomach."

With that Chief Regan blew his cool, tore up the arrest complaint, and ordered Papa, Mama and Mario out of the police station. Nick Molise wouldn't budge, his big fists clinging to the cell bars. Three police rapped his knuckles as they jumped him, pushed him down the hall, and flung him into the street.

Here a fight flared between the old man and Mario as they rolled down the station steps and across the sidewalk to the gutter. The police tore them apart and would have booked them for disturbing the peace, but the chief, anxious to avoid further involvement, ordered his staff inside and the door bolted. And then my brother Mario, a peaceful man of forty, a trifle bombastic but hardly a brawler, took an unmerciful clouting from the old man, for Mario would as soon strike our Lord Himself as his own father.

The dreadful imbroglio ended with Mario slumped in the gutter, holding a bloody handkerchief to his nose, while Mama cried out to a gathering of San Elmo citizens watching the spectacle in silence and careful not to become involved.

In truth, this wasn't the first time the head of the Molise family had made a fool of himself in public. Only a few months before he had taken on a young bartender at the Onyx Club who punched him soundly and threw him into the street, whereupon he had heaved a bench through the saloon's window. The ruckus cost me a hundred, which I paid by check and, thanks to Regan, the matter never went to court.

In fact, over the years, on street corners, in saloons and polling places, Nick Molise had engaged in so many disputes that the family's good name was grievously compromised in the town. Even so, the citizens manifested tolerance and good will, for everyone liked the old man and enjoyed his explosive ways.

Cranky, noisy, taking advantage of their patience, drunk a good deal of the time, he had free rein in San Elmo, and at night people heard him lurching home along deserted streets, singing bad renditions of "O Sole Mio," people untroubled in their beds, saying, "There goes old Nick," and smiling, for he was a part of their lives.

Everyone, that is, except his sons Mario and Virgil. Manager of the Loan Department of the First National Bank, my brother Virgil was convinced that Papa's antics had ruined his banking career. Mario blamed his father for denying him a college education as well as the opportunity to become a bricklayer and stonemason. As for my sister Stella, she never ceased her disapproval of the old man — his drinking, his gambling, his wenching, and his cruelty toward our mother. She had an uncanny ability to intimidate him. A flash of her dark eyes and he cringed like a dog. Though she loved him, she despised him too, determined to remember all that Mama tried but failed to forget.

But to return to my brother's telephone call.

After his assault on Mario, my father stood on the steps of the police station and delivered a violent speech to the gathering crowd. He denounced the treachery of his own son for having him arrested, he called the police criminals for abusing a law-abiding citizen, and he castigated Mama as an insane old fool who persecuted an honorable man who only wished to live in peace.

Mario gagged in disgust as he told of Mama's shrieks of denial while she moved frantically toward the onlookers, snatching at their sleeves as they drew away and she went on and on about the lipstick on her husband's underwear. "You think that's the way for a married man to behave?" she beseeched. "Who does his laundry, cleans his house, cooks his meals? Is that the thanks I get — lipstick from the mouth of some slut?"

The crowd dispersed in horror. Even Papa fled the vulgar scene, dashing down Oak Street and across the Southern Pacific tracks to the Café Roma, a hideaway for elderly Italian males.

Bloodied and embarrassed, Mario helped Mama into the truck.

As fate would have it, the battery was dead and the car refused to start. Like refugees of war, mother and son trudged across town to the redwood house on Pleasant Street. Later Mario picked up a loan battery from the Shell station and returned to the truck. The police had affixed a parking ticket to his windshield. He drove back to Pleasant Street.

Arriving home, Mama began packing a suitcase, determined to board a bus to Denver, where she planned to move in with her sister Carmelina. She knew she would be welcome, for Carmelina, our ancient aunt, detested my father and had made a lifetime hobby of sabotaging his marriage.

In the midst of my mother's packing, my sister Stella and my brother Virgil stormed into the house, having heard from many sources of the wild scene in front of the police station. My mother, never one to waste a dramatic improvisation in the presence of her children, promptly passed out on the kitchen floor, thus heading off the hasty and ill-conceived bus ride over the Sierras to Denver, a journey she would have found exceedingly difficult, for she suffered from backache and chronic urinary frequency.

A sniff of crushed garlic against her nostrils brought Mama around, and with the pluck of a Saint Bernadette she began to stagger about, bringing wine and Genoa tarts to the table, where a discussion of her problems with Papa ensued.

These dialogues, I well remembered, had taken place frequently over the years and had never come to anything fruitful. Old bones were excavated and strewn about, everyone talked at the top of his voice, and the emotional mess left only bitterness and gloom. Like the mystery of the Immaculate Conception, the problem of my father was simply insoluble, defying logic, making no sense at all.

My brother Virgil was in a special frenzy. The police station spectacle had been witnessed by his employer, J. K. Eicheldorn, president of the bank, and the distinguished first citizen of San Elmo was not pleased. Calling Virgil into his office, J. K. asserted bluntly that the antics of Mr. and Mrs. Molise were a slur upon the bank's reputation, and if they continued Virgil's position would be in jeopardy.

Pounding the kitchen table, Virgil wept as he accused Mama and Papa of being out of their heads, socially irresponsible and doddering old fools who should be put away.

This brought more lamentations from my mother as she wrung her hands and implored Our Lord to come and get her. Mario rushed to her defense, cursing Virgil, damning him as a stuffed shirt and a coward, deserting his own parents for the sake of social approval.

Gifted with a vicious tongue, Virgil quickly put Mario in his place by calling him "the lowest form of human being known to man — a railroad brakeman." It was too much. Mario struck Virgil in the mouth, and Virgil retaliated with a blow to the nose. Then they were grappling all over the kitchen, overturning chairs, toppling pots and pans from the pantry, Mama shrieking and Stella dashing to her house across the alley to get the help of her husband, John DiMasio, the bricklayer. By the time she returned with John the fight was over. Virgil was gone and Mario stood over the kitchen sink, ministering to a bloody nose for the second time on that eventful day.

Calm was restored, but Mama quickly stirred things up again. "What am I going to do with that dirty old goat?" she asked. It was an ugly way to provoke a subject that nobody wanted to discuss anymore, and it was so repugnant to DiMasio that he walked out of the house. From the alley he called on Stella to get her ass home.

Stella ignored him. "Mama," she said, "you have no actual proof that Papa was unfaithful. It's all circumstantial evidence."

Mama threw up her hands in shock. "Circumstantial evidence? Oh, Mother of God, protect me from my own children!"

She staggered into the bedroom and returned with the telltale shorts, pushing aside dishes and glasses and spreading the underwear over the center of the checkered tablecloth like a shameless centerpiece. The reddish smears staining the crotch were quite visible.

"It was lipstick sure as hell," Mario said over the telephone. "The kiss of some tart."

My sister Stella, married to her wayward, urbane bricklayer, insisted that the stain was from a red mouthwash she had seen in the bathroom. "That's all it is — plain mouthwash."

It was as if she had felled Mama with a club. Her face dropped forward on the table, her head thudding.

"I'm so tired," she moaned. "Oh, Blessed Lord, deliver me from this cross. I just can't take it anymore. Fifty-one years I've done my best, and now I've run out of patience. I want out. I want some peace in my old age. I want a divorce."

She leaped to her feet, electrified by her own words. "Divorce! Divorce!" She raced through the house and out the front door, down the porch steps, and into the middle of the street, screaming at the top of her voice, pulling at her hair.

"Divorce, divorce! I'm getting a divorce!"

Doors opened on both sides of the street and wives spilled out onto front porches, young wives and old, watching in silence and sympathy, the problems in the Molise household having been theirs too for many years.

Next door Mrs. Romano shook her finger approvingly.

"You're doing the right thing, Maria. Get rid of the old bastard!"

Mario and Virgil dashed from the house, seized Mama, and hustled her back up the porch steps and through the front door.

Center stage and inspired, Mama snatched up the telephone and called Harry Anderson, the family lawyer. "Draw up the papers, Harry. I mean it this time. I'm divorcing the animal."

Anderson tried to discourage her as usual, and Stella tore the telephone from her grasp, but Mama seized it again. "I'll sign anything, Harry. Get the papers ready. I want the house. He can't come in here anymore. Let him sleep in the tool shed. Tell him to come and get his clothes. I'm throwing all his junk in the alley, and that goes for his dirty underwear. The concrete mixer in the backyard, I want it moved by tomorrow or I'll give it to the Good Will!"

Anderson agreed to meet her at his office the following day. "So that's where it's at," Mario finished off, his voice trembling and desolate. "I can't believe it, Henry! The end of our family. They won't live a month without each other."

"It won't happen," I told him.

"You've got to save them, Henry. You're the only one who can."

I could understand why they were afraid of this ludicrous divorce, of what chaos it would create in their quiet small-town lives. They were no longer in their youth, their hopes for the future were exhausted, and they were already burdened enough with swarms of children crammed into three-bedroom stucco houses with small backyards, a lemon tree in the corner, tomato vines up the back fence, and teen-age daughters in misery for a bedroom of their own. If divorced, where would my mother and father go? Who had spare bedrooms to house them?

True, Mama had queasy, halfhearted plans to share her sister's flat in Denver, but such a ménage wouldn't last forty-eight hours, for the daft Carmelina (always in the same black shawl and dress) was a kinky arthritic confined to a wheelchair, in need of constant attention, and she was an even worse tyrant than Nick Molise. A couple of nights in Carmelina's unventilated apartment and Mama would flee back to San Elmo, to live alone in the crumbling shingle house on Pleasant Street, careless about gas jets in the kitchen stove and prone to falling asleep with the wall furnace going full blast. My old man may have been a poor excuse for a husband, but he at least had sense enough to lower the furnace and open a window in order to survive the night.

What of him? Where would he go after a divorce?

"You're the oldest son," Mario said. "He's your problem."

"It cannot happen," I wearily assured him. "A husband and

wife bonded together for fifty-one years of marriage are insepar-
able, like Siamese twins. If they split they die, and they know it."

"I told you — she's seeing the lawyer tomorrow."

"It won't happen. She'll see him, but it'll be for show. Nothing
serious."

"Listen, Henry. You've got that nice house at Redondo Beach,
all those bedrooms, your kids are grown and gone, you're sitting
pretty, you've got space, and we were wondering, me and Stella,
if you could help us until this crisis is over, maybe take the old
man off our hands for a few days."

"I'll take them both."

"You can't. They're talking about divorce. They'll fight all the
time. You don't want that."

"I'll take them anyway, married or divorced."

"Talk it over with Harriet."

"What's to talk about? I'm master of my own house."

"Just old Nick. Give me your word."

"Mario, this is a collect call. We've been talking for an hour, and
it's costing me."

The phone flooded with the swoosh of his anger. "A crisis like
this and all you think about is the phone bill! Is money that
important? Don't you have any sympathy for the woman who
brought you into the world, or the man who raised you by the
sweat of his brow, bought your shoes and clothes, put bread in
your mouth and sent you to school? You think you'd be a writer
today if it wasn't for those two wonderful people? You always
were number one. What about me and Virgil and Stella? You
think we enjoyed it seeing you always the favorite? You think I
enjoyed it, wearing your hand-me-down shirts and socks? I
woulda worn your pants too, only you're so fuckin' short they
barely covered my knees. You think I forgot who got the bike, and
not me or Virgil? We had to sleep together, me and that farting
Virgil. But not you! Oh, no, you had your own little room on the
back porch with your books and your typewriter and the special
light. I won't forget that, Henry! I never forget anything! I know

how you live, you phony. Laying around on that beach all day long, playing like you're somebody important just because you're a writer, writing bullshit lies about your family while I slave like a wetback in the yards, eight, ten hours a day — and for what? For nothing but trouble and debts while you're out of it and far away, listening to the waves, and when I call to tell you that your mother and father are getting a divorce, the best you can do is beef about the phone bill. Okay, buster. Drop dead!"

He hung up with a crash.

I found Harriet under a blanket on the little porch above the beach. Mounds of fog meandered toward the shore like a herd of wandering polar bears. The night was cold and moonless; even the stars would have no part of it. I slipped under the blanket beside her and related the conversation with my brother.

"Hurray for your mother," Harriet said. "She should have divorced the old bastard fifty years ago."

"She's a devout Catholic. There won't be a divorce."

"I hope she does. Think of it, free from that old satyr at last."

"Harriet, she's seventy-four . . ."

"She'll make out just fine. There's Stella and your brothers, and of course you'll help out too. It's your duty."

"What happens to Nick?"

"What's the difference? He's always been a bachelor anyway."

I paused to consider an innocuous way of saying it, but there really wasn't any, so I simply said, "I'm thinking of bringing him down here for a while."

Her body stiffened under the blanket. She turned and studied me with a startled glance as paleness washed the color from her face. Peering into the tunnels of her eyes was like staring at an arctic landscape, frozen and silent as her breathing stopped.

"It's getting chilly," she said. "I think I'll fix a hot drink."

She must have fixed quite a few, for as I sat at my typewriter an hour later she blossomed in the doorway like a ghost, wearing a white robe and a wavering smile, a cigarette in one hand, a drink in the other.

"I've changed my mind," she said, addressing my stare. "A divorce between your mother and father makes no sense at all."

"Of course not."

"You'd better go up to San Elmo, Henry. Talk to them."

"Did you ever try to talk to my father?"

"Your mother. After all, it's her idea."

"Are you changing your mind because you don't want my father down here?"

"You're damn right. You better get up there before they do something stupid. They're both weird and you know it."

She was right. We were an impulsive, unpredictable clan, prone to rash decisions and terrible remorse. Even if my mother dropped the divorce idea, my father might take revenge by leaving home and arriving without notice in Redondo Beach. Grimly Harriet crossed the room to the telephone, the extension cord uncoiling as she brought the instrument to my desk.

"Call your brother. Tell him you're coming."

I dialed San Elmo. Mario answered so swiftly his hand must have been on the receiver, as if expecting the call.

"What the hell do you want now?" he snarled.

I told him I would fly up in the morning.

"What is this, some kind of a trick?"

"No trick. I think I should come up, that's all. I'll take the eleven o'clock flight. Meet me in Sacramento at noon."

"How come you changed your mind, Henry?"

"Reasons."

"Harriet?" He laughed. "It figures."

"Twelve o'clock. Sacramento airport."

"I'll be there."

I hung up and looked at Harriet. She smiled as she came toward me. She stood behind me with her arms around my waist.

"Thank you," she said, her hands slipping past my navel and into my pants. She fondled me, pressed the tip of her tongue into my ear, gently squeezed and stroked me with ten wise, evocative fingers fashioning a fugue for fucking on my flute, and when she breathed, "Let's do it," I hurried after her into the bedroom, struggling to peel off my jeans, fearful that the music would stop suddenly as it often had these past months.

Like two serpents we writhed around each other, her breath coming in gasps. "Do something for me!" she begged. And thinking perhaps she might want me to eat her, I said, "Yes, anything, honey. Anything!"

"While you're in San Elmo, promise you'll pay my mother a visit. She's changed, Henry. She likes you now."

That did it. The flute pooped out, the music stopped, and I was raging.

"No," I said, pushing myself away, rising from the bed.

"What's the matter with you?"

I was ashamed to tell her the old bitterness still festered in me. How could a mature man, a supposedly compassionate person, stark naked, turn and say to his wife, "I hate your mother." With my clothes on I might have said it; instead, I went down the hall to the linen closet, snatched a blanket, and spent the night on the divan.

Next morning we passed one another in the hall.

"Good morning," I said.

"What's good about it?"

I went into the bathroom to shave. The face in the mirror was that of an escaped lunatic. The days no longer brought peace but ugliness — the veins in my eyes, the beginning of jowls. I glanced at the rumpled bed where we had lain in flawed love, the crushed pillows, the twisted sheets. I remembered seeing them exactly that way in my parents' bedroom when I was seven, and hating my father for it, for the stale smell of his cigar, and his work pants lying grotesquely on the floor, and the desire to kill him.

2

WE CHOSE to be silent as I drove to the airport — twenty minutes of stinking nitrous oxides along the Coast Highway, Harriet sulking furiously in the corner, smoking one cigarette after another. Her smoking always amused me because she didn't inhale, she merely sucked the smoke into her mouth and popped it out of her nose, but fast, the cigarette almost catching fire.

Quietly, casually, she said, "May I tell you something about your father?"

"What?"

"Something I've never told you before."

"What's that?"

"Promise you won't repeat it."

"Oh, shit, Harriet . . ."

"He made a pass at me."

The revelation did nothing to me — it was like saying my father was a big wine drinker. I looked straight ahead, waiting for her to fill in the date and circumstance.

"Did you hear what I said?" she demanded. "I said Nick Molise, your father, made a pass at me."

"I heard you."

"You rotten son of a bitch. Is that all you have to say?"

"When did it happen?"

"On our wedding day. On the back porch of your mother's house."

It astonished me. Her face was a fury. The thing must have been bending her mind for years. I said, "You mean, like twenty-six years ago?"

"Does it matter *when?* It happened, that's all. I was your bride — his son's wife, in my wedding gown, on a sacred day in my life, and that dirty little bastard made a pass at me. Doesn't that mean anything to you?"

"I'm sorry, Harriet. I just can't seem to get worked up about it. Why didn't you tell me when it happened?"

"And spoil that lovely day?"

"Maybe it wasn't a pass. Maybe it was affection. I remember he drank a lot of champagne. Are you sure? What kind of a pass was it?"

"He pinched my derrière." (That was just like Harriet: she could always say "fuck" or "shit" but when it came to "ass" it was always "derrière" or "bottom.")

I laughed. "That wasn't a pass, it was a compliment. All Italians do that. I've pinched your ass a thousand times. It's fun."

"I don't want him around my house," she growled, her chest heaving. "He's a filthy old lecher with black Dago eyes that give me the creeps. I won't have him under my roof, and that's final."

Now the traffic was bumper to bumper as it eased into the airport complex. Sulking and dangerous, Harriet exploded another cloud of uninhaled cigarette smoke, her eyes slit like a cat's.

"Do me a favor when you get there."

"Be glad to."

"Visit my mother."

"Never."

I pulled to the curb at Western Airlines and got out. Harriet slid to the driver's side. I kissed her cheek that tasted like a cold rock.

"Will you see my mother, please?"

"No."

Her toe hit the throttle and I was almost decapitated as the car spurted out into traffic.

3

It was a comfortable flight, serene and reflective, up the San Joaquin Valley, following the river, cruising low over green farms, passing familiar towns — Bakersfield, Fresno, Turlock, Stockton — a time to sip good beer and float back into the past, to orient one's self to the emotion of returning home. My thoughts were of my father, for he was an old man now; his days were thinning out, and the less time remaining the more rebellious he got, whereas it seemed that my mother, despite her failing eyesight, rheumatic fingers and backache, would be with us for many years to come.

My father would have been a happier man without a family. Were it not for his four children he would have been divorced and long gone to other towns. He loved Stockton, which was full of Italians, and Marysville, where one could play the Chinese lottery day and night. His children were the nails that crucified him to my mother. No kids and he would have been as free as a bird.

He did not like us particularly, and certainly he did not love us at all. We were just ordinary kids, plain and undistinguished, and he expected more. We were chores that had to be done, not a rich harvest, not asparagus or figs or dates, but humbler fare, potatoes and corn and beans, and he was stuck with the toil of it, cursing and kicking clods until the crops matured.

He was a hard-nosed, big-fisted mountain man from Abruzzi, short, five feet seven, wide as a door, born in a part of Italy where poverty was as spectacular as the surrounding glaciers, and any child who survived the first five years would live to eighty-five. Of course, not many reached the age of five. He and my Aunt Pepina, now eighty and living in Denver, were the only two out of thirteen who had survived. That way of life gave my father his toughness. Bread and onions, he used to boast, bread and onions — what else does a man need? That was why my whole life has been a loathing of bread and onions. He was more than the head of the family. He was judge, jury and executioner, Jehovah himself.

Nobody crossed him without a battle. He disliked almost everything, particularly his wife, his children, his neighbors, his church, his priest, his town, his state, his country, and the country from which he emigrated. Nor did he give a damn for the world either, or the sun or the stars, or the universe, or heaven or hell. But he liked women.

He also liked his work and half a dozen paisani who, like himself, were Italians in the dictator mold. He was a flawless craftsman whose imagination and intelligence seemed centered in his marvelously strong hands, and though he called himself a building contractor I came to regard him as a sculptor, for he could shape a rock into man or beast. He was a superb, swift, neat bricklayer as well as an excellent carpenter, plasterer and concrete builder.

He had great contempt for himself, yet was proud and even conceited. Nick Molise believed that every brick he laid, every stone he carved, every sidewalk and wall and fireplace he built, every gravestone he fashioned, belonged to posterity. He had a terrifying lust for work and a bitter squint at the sun which, in his view, moved too fast across the sky. To finish a job brought him deep sadness. His love for stone was a pleasure more fulfilling than his passion for gambling, or wine, or women. He usually worked far beyond quitting time, even into darkness, and he had a bad reputation among hod carriers and helpers for overworking them. He was always in bad standing with the bricklayers' union.

The town of San Elmo was his Louvre, his work spread out for the world to see. He was angry that the town did not recognize his talents. Had the city council awarded him a medal or a scroll it might have changed his entire life. What the hell, every year the Chamber of Commerce passed out commendations to noteworthy citizens; they gave Cramer, the Ford distributor, a scroll for Man of the Year, and they gave another to G. K. Laurel, the druggist — so how come they never took notice of what Nick Molise had done for their asshole town?

A consistent breadwinner, my father had a problem — he never brought the bread home. The poker game at the Elks Club had sucked up thousands of dollars over the years. I remember him counting out seven hundred and eighty dollars for the completion of a stone house, piles of tens and twenties on the kitchen table as he wet a pencil with his tongue and marked the numbers on a piece of paper. When my mother asked for money to buy groceries he offered her five dollars, his face wincing in pain as she stuffed it into her apron. His credit status among merchants was disgraceful, for he never paid his bills unless backed to the wall. He didn't believe in banking. He liked the sensuality of a big roll of greenbacks in his pocket. He flashed the money, a big shot, and predators in the saloons licked their chops, waiting for him to take a seat at the gaming tables. The Elks Club, the Onyx, the Café Roma, Kelly's — all the dives beside the railroad tracks on Atlantic Street. Nick drifted from one to another, trying to change his luck — poker at the Elks, blackjack at Kelly's, pinochle at the Café Roma, and finally, down to his last dollar or so, a penny hearts game in the lobby of the Elmo Hotel. Tenacious, tireless, expectant, he hung in there until his pockets were empty. Then he stumbled home, weary and debauched from wine, falling upon the bed, where my mother pulled off his clothes and searched his pockets, finding nails, matches, the stub of a pencil, but never so much as a dime.

Next morning he was on the job an hour before his fellow workers arrived, sweat oozing through his shirt as he screened sand or mixed mortar, or hefted a hod of brick to the scaffold, dangerous as a dog with distemper, sick with the nausea of his own affliction. Why this passion for gambling? Virgil believed it stemmed from his poverty in childhood. But that was too easy an explanation. I believed it was his rage at the world, his desire for triumph over the Establishment, his immigrant sense of being an outsider.

But he never had a chance, for he was a miserable player, desperate, terrifying, playing a pair of deuces like a pat hand, never backing down, raising and reraising the bet until his last chip was pushed into the pot. Of course luck was with him sometimes, when he won everything in sight and broke up the game. Exultant, laughing, he bought drinks on the house and hurried off down Atlantic Street to another game, for he could not quit. He had to go on until his final destruction, like a man determined to sacrifice himself to a fatal passion. Many was the night when Mama, knowing he carried a large sum of money after the completion of a job, sent us to search for him in one of the saloons. We never got to him, for he had established a rule with the house man: his kids were not allowed in the back room where the gamblers gathered.

Sometimes in the evenings after supper my father would trap one of us boys as we sat on the front porch and he came swinging out the door, pausing to light a long black Toscanelli and snapping, ''Okay, kid. On your feet. Let's go.''

''Where to?''

''Follow me.''

Down the street he'd move on quick feet as I hurried to keep pace. It was the Grand Tour, the complete works of Nick Molise.

Everybody took it except Mama and my sister. Apparently he regarded it as inappropriate for women.

In those days San Elmo was a town of twelve thousand split by railroad tracks down the middle, the business district and the aristocrats on one side, the railroad machine shops, the round-house and the peasants on the other. My father's first stop on the tour was across town in the neighborhood of the rich, where the public library was situated, a white brick structure, pure New England, with four stone columns above a cascade of red sandstone steps.

Pausing across the street, hands on hips, his face softened reverently as he stared at the building.

''There she is, kid. Isn't she pretty? You know who built her?''

''You did, Papa.''

''Not bad. Not bad at all.''

''It's a beauty, Papa.''

''Last a thousand years.''

''At least.''

''Look at that stone, those steps. They flow like water.''

''Great.''

''Hell of a thing.''

He'd drop a hand on my shoulder. ''Come on, kid. I got something else to show you.''

Then two blocks down Maywood to the Methodist church with its stone steeple and the open bell tower, the ivy-covered stone walls. Five minutes of silent, ritualistic admiration, gazing up at the steeple, the air magical with my father's joy, his eyes dancing at his handiwork, his face suffused with contentment.

''I did it,'' he'd assert. ''Yes, sir. I did it.''

''You sure did.''

Off and running again, chasing his heels. The City Hall. The Bank of California. Municipal Water and Power, Spanish-style, with adobe colonnades and a red tile roof. Haley's Mortuary. The Criterion Theatre. The Fire Department, all red brick and spot-less, with expanses of flawless concrete. On to San Elmo High

School, with respectful pauses at places of interest — winding concrete walkways, drinking fountains.

"Stop, kid." He'd block me with his hand. "Down at your feet. What does it look like?"

"Sidewalk."

"Whose sidewalk?"

"Yours."

"Wrong. It's the people's. Your father built it for them, to keep their feet dry."

San Elmo High. Red brick. Immense stone stairs, and Papa, hands behind his back, squinting through cigar smoke as he gazed at what we kids came to call "the invisible marvel."

"Notice anything?"

I'd shake my head. Just a damned school.

"Look careful. You can't see it, you'll never see it, but I'll show it to you."

My eyes would roll to the inscription across the front of the building. SAN ELMO HIGH SCHOOL. 1936.

"Not *that!* " he'd say, annoyed. "Look at the building! What's special about it?"

"You built it."

"What else? What is it you don't see?"

"How do I know if I don't see it?"

"You can — if you use your head."

I'd move up to the school wall and touch it here and there, scanning it up and down and across, bored to death with his ego trip, playing out a silly game.

"Can't see anything."

"What you see is a building that's been through four earthquakes. Now, look close and tell me what you can't see."

"Dead people."

He'd shake his head in disgust. "You dumb jackass! I'm talking about *cracks!* Earthquake cracks. Find me a crack in those walls. Go ahead."

"I can't, because there aren't any."

23

"So, then. What is it in that building that's plain to see because you can't see it?"

"A crack."

"Why?"

"Because you built it."

He'd dig into his pocket. "Here's a quarter. Don't spend it all in one place.,

I'd take it and run, free at last.

Other times it was the graveyard tour at Valhalla Cemetery, just outside the city limits. It could happen unexpectedly on a Sunday afternoon, an agonizing ordeal if you were thirteen and scheduled to pitch against the Nevada City Tigers at two o'clock and it was already one-thirty, and he was oblivious to your uniform, your glove and your cleats as you followed him around, knowing the ball park was ten blocks across town.

Valhalla Cemetery was crowded with my father's white marble angels, their wings unfolded, their arms and long fingers outstretched, hawk-faced and grim, a fearsome thrust about them like vultures protecting carrion. Wherever they perched, one got the feeling that they had already desecrated the graves.

Down the cypress-lined path was the enormous bust of Mayor Hal Shriner, stern and iron-jawed, the menacing, cruel countenance of a crooked politician staring down at you from a pedestal above the sunken grave, his eyes empty, a few bird droppings on his stony hair. My father would remove his hat and stare in wonder, like a man enchanted by Michelangelo's David, while I'd pound my mitt in a frenzy.

"Nine years he's been dead," my father would muse. "Now he's all gone, finished." His eyes met the mayor's. "Hello, Mayor, you old son of a bitch. How they treating you down there?"

I would stare out over a sea of tombstones and groan. There still seemed acres to traverse. The whole world had turned into a graveyard. What a way to warm up before a ball game! He knew why I seethed and festered, pawing the gravel with my spiked shoes, he *knew*, but he didn't give a damn as he solemnly moved along the path to the gravestone of old Loretta Stevens, the librarian, fashioned like an open book, her vital statistics chiseled on a stony page.

4

MY OLD MAN had never wanted children. He had wanted apprentice bricklayers and stonemasons. He got a writer, a bank teller, a married daughter, and a railroad brakeman. In a sense he tried to shape his sons into stonemasons the way he shaped stone, by whacking it. He failed, of course, for the more he hammered at us, the further he drove us from any love of the craft. When we were kids a great dream possessed Nick Molise, a glimpse of a glorious future lit up in his brain: MOLISE AND SONS, STONEMASONS.

We sons had his brown eyes, his thick hands, his fireplug stature, and he assumed we were naturally blessed with the same devotion to stone, the same dedication to long hours of backbreaking toil. He envisioned a modest beginning in San Elmo, then expansion of operations to Sacramento, Stockton and San Francisco.

The only son who made a serious attempt to share my father's dream was Mario, who gave it a heroic try after graduating from high school. Since Papa was dealing with a raw apprentice and not a member of the union, he put Mario through a test past all endurance, working him from early morning until after sunset six

26

days a week, at paltry wages paid only when the spirit moved him. He felt that Mario should actually be working for nothing, just for the privilege of having such an illustrious maestro. The apprentice period should last five years, he thought, but in Mario's case, since his son was so stupid and difficult to instruct, the training period should be extended to seven years.

"Okay!" Mario would keep saying. "But teach me something! I might as well be at Folsom, breaking rocks."

"That's the idea," Papa would say. "First we break you down, so that you're nothin'. Then we build you up and up, until you can raise your head and tell the world you're a first-class bricklayer, the son of Nicholas Molise."

"Aw, bullshit!"

Three months into his apprenticeship Mario had an offer to play professional baseball with the San Francisco Seals of the Pacific Coast League. At seventeen he was already an extraordinary pitcher, had thrown two no-hit games for the San Elmo High School team, and was the star left-hander for the town team. Playing baseball was the one talent that lifted Mario above the crowd, the passion of his life. Though graduated from high school, he was still a minor, so the San Francisco management needed parental consent before signing him up.

Mama was eager to sign, but the old man refused. Mario was too young, he insisted, and besides, baseball was a foolish way to earn a living. Five, six years and you were through, a nothing, a ditch-digger. Better that he should have an honorable profession, that of a mason, building with brick and stone, than earning money playing a kid game with no future.

God, what a brutal time: we fought him for weeks — Stella, Virgil and I — pleading with him to give Mario his chance, yelling at him, then refusing to speak to him at all. But he was an Abruzzi goat with poised evil horns and he would not relent. He knew what was best for his son, and someday Mario would thank him. Needless to say, there was no gratitude in Mario's soul, only bitterness and fury.

Gritting his teeth, he went back to the rocks and cement, patiently awaiting the day when he would be eighteen and beyond Papa's legal hold on his baseball future. But it never happened. The New York Giants moved to the Bay Area that winter and the San Francisco Seals were no more. Mario's big opportunity vanished in the upheaval. Suddenly he was a nobody once more. True, my father had taught him the rudiments of laying brick, but he was still an apprentice, still made to grovel and crawl at the old man's will, the seeds of patricide sprouting in his gut. The moment he heard there was no deal with the Seals, Mario leaped from the scaffold of the building my father was constructing and walked away. Papa was shocked and unforgiving. For years he refused to speak to Mario, even crossing the street when he saw his son approaching. In fact, Mario crossed the street when he saw my father approaching.

"He sold me out," Papa would say. "He deserted his own father."

Sunday afternoons in summer, my father sat in the grandstand heckling Mario as he pitched semipro ball for the town team against Marysville, Yuba City, Grass Valley, Auburn and Lake Tahoe. Full of beer on those hot afternoons, he was a one-man rooting section, cheering the opposition to clobber his own flesh and blood. "Knock him out of there! Knock his brains out!" he shouted to the batters facing Mario.

I sat with the old man in a crucial game between San Elmo and Yuba City. In the last of the ninth, with the score tied, Mario hit a home run to win the league championship. As he rounded third base to the cheers of the locals, my enraged father rushed from the grandstand and tackled the grinning Mario as he rounded third base. The police dragged him off the field and Mario got up and trotted home with the winning run.

5

THE JET HIT the Sacramento runway on schedule and the passengers unhooked their safety belts. I was first to disembark as a gust of September heat blasted off the concrete runway, shimmering like an unfocused television screen. I had forgotten the heat of the Sacramento Valley. Now I knew I was home again.

My brother Mario was not at the reception gate, where a few people had gathered to meet the Los Angeles flight. I went inside the refrigerated depot and sat down to wait. After fifteen minutes I walked out into the parking area to look for Mario's truck. There was no sign of Mario and the heat was crushing. I ducked inside the waiting room again, found the cool, dark bar, and ordered beer. By one-thirty I began to doubt that Mario would show up. I dialed his home in San Elmo and his wife Peggy answered. Her voice always had the breathless quality of a mother pursuing children.

"Who'd you say this was?"

"Henry Molise. Your brother-in-law."

"Well, for God's sake. Henry Molise! What brings you up here, Henry? Are you still writing those shitty novels? The last one made me vomit. I burned it so the children wouldn't be contaminated. Lord, what a way to make a living!" (The novel concerned a young railroad brakeman who deserted his wife and children for a career in professional baseball. There was no way for Peggy to like it.)

"Is Mario there, Peggy?"

"Maybe. Why?"

"I want to talk to him."

"It's your smart-ass brother," I heard her call out. "Do you want to talk to him?"

There was a roar in the background, a sporting event of some kind on television. After a long time the volume of the crowd noises was reduced and Mario spoke.

"Hi, Henry. What's up? You watching the game?"

"Game? What game? You were supposed to meet me at the airport."

"Forget it. Don't come up. I was going to call you. Everything's okay. They made up. All that talk about a divorce — it didn't mean a thing."

"You jerk! Why didn't you let me know?"

"I meant to, Henry. It slipped my mind."

"Come and get me."

"Get you? Where are you?"

"Sacramento airport."

"You mean, you came up?"

"How the hell could I be at the Sacramento airport if I didn't come up? I flew up, Mario! I'm here, in a phone booth, talking to you. Come and get me!"

He moaned.

"Can't do it, Henry. It's the Giants and the Dodgers. Bobby Murcer's at bat with two on. For God's sake, Henry, go someplace and find a television set! Hurry! The game's just started!"

"You rat!"

"Sorry, Henry. Tell you what: there's a bus to San Elmo at five. I'll pick you up at the depot."

I struggled for self-control.

"I don't want to see you again for the rest of my life," I told him. "But please. Do me a favor. Don't tell Mama and Papa I'm coming. I don't want them at the depot, waiting for me. I don't want any part of that scene. Okay?"

"Oh, shit," he said. "Murcer struck out."

I hung up and went back to my perch at the bar, depressed, frustrated. Mario was a born bungler. No wonder my father was always disgusted with him, always putting him down.

The voice over the public address system announced the next flight to Los Angeles. Suddenly I had a premonition of terrible problems in San Elmo and decided to fly back home. But as I hurried toward the embarkation gate my mind changed. I had come this far, so why not continue another eighteen miles and complete the journey? I owed it to my folks, if only for a few hours.

The airport bus took me into Sacramento, where I went to a movie, loafed around a bookstore, stopped in a bar for a beer and a few plays at the pinball game, and finally boarded a bus to San Elmo, altogether a most fruitful and rewarding day thanks to my wayward brother who had not only triggered the journey but had left me stranded at the end of it.

Coming into San Elmo down Main Street you could see that the town had changed, now that Highway 80 to the Sierras veered away from the city two miles north. San Elmo was isolated now, its lifeline cut, and the town was dying. Except for a few cars parked before the Safeway and Penney's, the main stem was deserted. Acme Billiards, where much of my early education for life was acquired, was closed down. So was the Ventura Theatre, where I saw every Elizabeth Taylor movie at least four times.

The bus turned right off Main Street, then left down the alley to the depot. I stepped down with two Chicanos and followed them inside the depot (formerly a clothing store), which had a few wooden benches fronting the windows looking out on Main Street. The ticket window was open but the depot was unattended. There were only two people in that desolate place. One was my mother, seated on a bench near the window, and the other was my father, seated on another bench as far away from her as possible.

Both saw me at the same time. My mother spoke first, crying out, "Henry, my boy!" and holding out her arms.

Though it was fearfully hot in the waning afternoon, she wore a heavy black coat with a fur-lined collar and hem. I knew that damned coat — we kids called it "the Colorado coat" — a hand-me-down from Aunt Carmelina thirty years ago, a flashy, almost whorish coat, absurdly draping my small, gray-haired mother. Beneath was a gingham housedress. I pulled her into my arms and kissed her hot face and smelled the scent of Italian spices always present in her hair.

"Thank God," she breathed, clinging to me. "Oh, thank God! All I wanted was to see my dear son one last time."

Her body twitched, then melted suddenly in my arms, her head thrown back, her mouth open, her eyes closed. She only weighed about a hundred and three pounds, but it was dead weight and hard to control, and I floundered with her, yelling at my father for help.

"Leave her go," he scowled, a little black cigar in his mouth. "Leave her fall on the floor."

But he crossed quickly to us, taking her like a sack of grain and hustling her to a bench, mumbling, "Son of a bitchen woman, why don't somebody put her out of her misery?" Splotches of angry blood bloated his neck and smoke from the black cigar stung his eyes.

Mama lay spread out as if unconscious, eyes closed, mouth open, one hand primly tugging her dress below the knee. Her stockings were held up by sleeve garters. I recognized them: they were discards from the old man's wardrobe.

"It's nothin'," Papa said. "Same old thing. Just nothin'."

"Water," Mama moaned.

I looked about for a water fountain.

"There ain't any in here," Papa said.

I ran out on Main Street and down four doors to the Colfax Café and asked the waitress for a glass of water. When I got back to the depot my mother was sitting up, her face thrown back as Papa bopped himself disgustedly at the side of his head. I put the paper cup to Mama's lips and she sipped the water timidly, like a kitten. It revived her with remarkable swiftness. Quickly she smiled with alert brown eyes as she studied me.

"You don't look well, Henry. Doesn't she treat you good?"

"She treats me fine, just fine. You feeling better now?"

"It's my heart, Henry. It won't be long now. I'm ready to go any time. I've had a terrible life. He kicked me. He choked me. He's like a wild animal now. You don't know what I have to put up with. He's strange, Henry. I'm afraid to go to bed at night."

Papa slumped down on the bench and let his body grow limp, wearily shaking his head as he stared at the bare wooden floor. I glanced at him commiseratingly and our eyes met.

"You don't know, kid," he said. "You'll never know the half of it."

This brought a moan from my mother. I took her hot dry hand.

"You rest a while. I'll call a taxi."

She shook her head. "Taxi costs fifty cents."

"Taxi went outa business two years ago," Papa said.

"Call Stella," I told him. "She'll come in her car."

"Nothin' wrong with that woman. Let her walk."

It was said quietly and truthfully, I was sure, but it was cruel nevertheless, for an old lady was entitled to her whims, especially my mother, who possessed little else. She struggled to get to her feet.

"I'll try," she said.

I put my arm around her. "I can't," she sighed, easing down on the bench again.

"She's lying," Papa said.

"Goddamn it! Call Stella!"

His face dropped in embarrassment. Blunt as he was to others, he could not bear it when anyone spoke harshly to him. His mustache was white now, his hair a brownish gray, like autumn leaves. He had the apple cheeks of the inveterate Chianti drinker and his brown eyes were cobwebbed with minute red veins. After a moment of brooding silence he crossed to the pay phone bolted to the wall, moving quickly but with a faint limp, as if pain pinched the soles of his feet. Though he still looked very strong, the patina of vitality was gone from his movements. He had lost weight and the seat of his khaki trousers drooped sadly.

He inserted a coin into the phone and began to dial, at the same time pronging his middle and index finger toward my mother, a peasant gesture of ill will.

Watching him, she whispered, "Can I tell you something, Henry?" I saw her eyes shining with cunning innocence.

"Yes?"

"Your father's losing his mind."

I said I didn't think so, that he was the same.

"Stella don't answer," Papa said from the phone.

The coin returned and he began to dial again. Suddenly he was yelling, his mouth like a bulldog's, snarling into the instrument, his fist shaking to emphasize his threats.

"I'll kill you!" he shouted. "I'll break every bone in your body. I'm warning you, keep away!"

It was madness, total frenzy.

"You see?" my mother said, pleased.

Certainly it was no way to speak to his own daughter. I crossed to the phone and lifted the receiver from his hand.

"Hello, Stella."

It wasn't Stella at all. It was Mario. He and my father were having their usual scholarly discourse.

"Listen, Henry," he implored. "Put a muzzle on that mad dog. All I said was, I can't leave now. It's the bottom of the seventh, Henry, and the Giants got two men on base. Oh God, man!

34

Matthews is on second, Rader's on third, and Murcer's stepping into the batter's box. Oh, sweet Jesus, it's now or never! I can't leave, Henry. I'm sorry . . . I'm sorry . . .''

"You still watching the same fucking game?'' I yelled.

"It's fantastic! It's the end of the world! Good-bye, Henry!'' He hung up.

I turned to my father. He was lighting a cigar stub. He flipped the match in disgust. "My son Mario!'' he grumbled; then he turned to Mama, "You ready to come home now, on your own two feet?''

"Let's all go home,'' she said cheerfully, scanning the barnlike room. "Where's the water closet?'' She saw the properly marked door and crossed to it without a trace of fatigue. Papa watched her enter. "Won't be long now,'' he reflected. "I give her a year at the most.''

"What are you talking about?''

He pressed a finger into his temple. "Her head. She's crazy.''

"You're both crazy.''

He flicked the remark aside as if dispersing a fly.

"Where's your suitcase?''

"Didn't bring any. I'm going back tonight.''

His red eyes seemed to catch fire. "No, you ain't. You stay a while.''

"I can't. Gotta work.''

"Work? You? What work?''

"My book.''

He snorted. "Book! You call that work?'' He threw his cigar at a spittoon and missed. "Then, go. Get out of here. Take the next bus. And don't come back.'' He spun around and marched for the door. I ran after him.

"Wait. I'll stay till tomorrow.''

I snatched at his arm, but he jerked it away and was gone, hurrying past the front window and down the street as Mama came out of the restroom. She got a flash of her husband hurrying across the street.

"What's he mad at now?"

I told her.

"Did he say anything about the job?"

"Job?"

"He knows. Let him tell you."

It sounded secretive, mysterious, conspiratorial, but she said no more as she stepped out onto the sidewalk. I squired her down the hot street to the intersection with the bank on the corner. She drew me toward the plate glass window and pointed to a desk, my brother Virgil's desk, with a bronze nameplate upon it: VIRGIL T. MOLISE — LOANS. At that hour the bank was closed.

"Look how neat he is," she said, pleased. "How clean he keeps his desk. Such a good boy."

"He always was a neat kid," I said. I almost added that he always was something of a prick too.

We crossed the street. She was perspiring and I made her take off the whorehouse coat. I slung it under my arm.

"I fixed you a nice dinner," she said. "Baked eggplant with ricotta cheese, gnocchi di latta, and veal. Remember the eggplant? It's your favorite."

"You knew I was coming."

"Mario phoned."

Oh, that Mario!

She took small quick steps, staying close to the line of shops on the shady side of Lincoln Street. Very few people were about in the infernal heat. Even the lobby of the Hotel Ritz, where railroad men liked to loaf in leather chairs, was deserted. A sick town. One had the feeling that bulldozers lurked at the city limits, waiting for the death rattle.

"Make your father see the doctor," she said. "At his age you never know."

"He looks fine. Thinner, but that's good."

"Too much wine. Up and down all night to the water closet. I bought some nice mozzarella. Tomorrow I'll fix some croquettes. Mario loves them."

We crossed the railroad tracks to the other side of Atlantic Street, the oldest part of town, with rotting brick stores, a street of a few Chinese shops, a laundry, a restaurant, and a dry goods store. The Café Roma was the last place on the dead-end street. "That's where he is," she said, looking toward it with a frown. "They have puttana upstairs."

"Really?"

There were always prostitutes upstairs above the Café Roma. After high school I used to go up there all the time, and I loved it especially on rainy winter afternoons, playing the jukebox and playing gin rummy for tricks with the girls.

I was there one night when a great commotion rumbled on the staircase, and I heard my own father yelling as the madam and three hookers pushed him into the alley for being drunk and obnoxious and broke. I was ashamed of him that night, and when the madam asked if I knew the man, I said no, I don't know the man, I never saw him before in my life; a crazy Dago, I said, they're all over town, they're all over town, and you could hear my father in the alley, yelling up at the window, "I'm going to the police! I'll have you shut down!"

Yes, I knew a great deal about the Café Roma and the rooms upstairs. I could still see the bare mattresses in the cribs and smell the cold loveless rooms and remember the sad, broken, stupid women, for San Elmo was in a prostitution circuit that included Marysville, Yuba City and Lodi, and when the syndicate sent a prostie down to San Elmo she had to be a pig, not even fit to work Yuba City, which was surely the end of the world.

Looking toward the neon sign blinking CAFÉ ROMA above the saloon, my mother's eyes heated with Christian righteousness. "Thank God you're all married. It keeps you out of those places."

I laughed and kissed her for this outrageous naiveté. "You go home now," I said. "I'll get Papa."

"Don't fight."

"No fighting."

"Tomorrow I'll make you a nice fritto misto with *scampi* and cauliflower."

"Beautiful."

"You still like new cabbage?"

"Love it."

"We'll see. Maybe day after tomorrow. And Sunday, ravioli." She was working it out in her mind, delicious little schemes to keep me there. I watched her mincing away on fast small feet, carrying her fur-trimmed coat.

6

THE ONLY CHANGE in the Café Roma in over a quarter of a century was the clientele. The old men I remembered were planted in the graveyard, replaced by a new generation of old men. Otherwise things were as usual. The long mahogany bar was the same and so were the two dusty, fly-specked Italian and American flags above it. A touch of the modern was displayed above the bar, a blowup of Marlon Brando as the Godfather, four feet square, in a frame of gold filigree.

The same propeller fan droned from the ceiling, spinning slowly enough not to disturb the warm air, with sportive flies landing on the propeller blades, enjoying a spin or two, then jumping off. Green shades over the front windows gave the dark interior an illusion of coolness, as did the fragrance of tap beer. But this aroma was knifed by the gut-slashing pungency of olive oil and rancid parmigiano cheese mixed with the piny tang of fresh sawdust deep on the floor.

Something else had changed: when I was a lad the patrons of the Café Roma spoke only Italian. Now the new breed of old cockers spoke English, the English of the street, but English all the same.

Eight or nine of them were crowded around a green felt table in the rear. The low-hanging lamp lit up five card players seated around the table, the others standing about, watching and kibitzing. My father was one of the spectators. They were a cranky, irascible, bitter gang of Social Security guys, intense, snarling, rather mean old bastards, bitter, but enjoying their cruel wit, their profanity and their companionship. No philosophers here, no aged oracles speaking from the depths of life's experience. Simply old men killing time, waiting for the clock to run down. My father was one of them. It came to me as a shock. I never thought of him that way until I saw him with his own kind. Now he looked even older than the gaffers around him.

I moved to Papa's side and said "Hi." He grunted. The baldheaded dealer never took his eyes off the cards as he spoke to my father.

"Friend of yours, Nick?"

"Nah. This is my kid Henry."

I recognized the dealer: Joe Zarlingo, a retired railroad engineer. Though he had not operated a train in ten years, he still wore striped overalls and an engineer's cap and sported all manner of colored pens and pencils in his bib pocket, as if serving notice that he was a very busy man.

I looked around and said "Hello" to everybody, and two or three answered with preoccupied growls, not bothering to look at me. Some I remembered. Lou Cavallaro, a retired brakeman. Bosco Antrilli, once the super at the telegraph office, the father of Nellie Antrilli, whom I seduced on an anthill in a field south of town in the dead of night (the anthill unseen, Nellie and I fully clothed, then screaming and tearing off our clothes as the outraged ants attacked us). Pete Benedetti, formerly postmaster. The game ended, the chips were drawn in, and the players finally took time to study me while Zarlingo shuffled the cards. They were not impressed.

"Which boy is this one, Nick?" Zarlingo asked.

"Writes books."

Zarlingo looked at me.

"Books, uh? What kind of books?"

"Novels."

"What kind?"

"Take your finger out of your ass and deal the cards," Antrilli said.

"Fuck you, you shit-kicker," Zarlingo fired back.

The profanity embarrassed my father, for in his mind I was still fourteen, the kid he dragged around on his tours, and he wanted to shield me from the vulgarity of his more mature friends. He whispered, "Come on," and drew me away, and I followed him out into the trembling sunshine.

"What you hanging around here for?" he said. "No place for you."

"Come on, Papa. I'm fifty years old. I've heard just about everything. I came to tell you I'm staying in town for a while."

It was like poking a stick into a hornet's nest. He squinted at me with his little hot red eyes. "Suit yourself, but don't do me no favors. I don't need any of you people. I been working since I was eight years old. I was laying stone on the streets of Bari twenty years before you were born, so don't think I can't do it myself."

"Do what?"

"Never mind."

I lifted my palms. "Papa, listen. Don't get sore. Let's get out of this heat and talk it over."

His hands plunged from one pocket to another until he found it — the stub of a black cigar. He struck a wooden match against his thigh and lit up, a cloud of white smoke burying his face.

"Okay. Let's talk business."

"Business?"

I followed him into the Roma to the bar. They had no hard liquor, only beer and wine. The bartender was the youngest man in the place, a kid of around forty-five, with hair down to the small of his back and a hip mustache that curled over his cheeks like quarter moons.

"Frank," Papa said. "This here's my son. Give him a beer." To me he said, "This is Frank Mascarini."

Frank drew me an overflowing stein from the tap. He served my father a decanter of Musso claret from one of the wine barrels beneath the bar. Papa took his decanter and a glass to one of the tables and I followed with the beer and we sat down. He sipped his wine thoughtfully. Whatever was on his mind, he was carefully tooling up to speak it.

Finally he said, "I got a chance to make some real money."

"Glad to hear of it."

He was a poor man but not a pauper. Social Security and checks from Virgil and me took care of him and Mama. They lived frugally but well, for my mother could make a meal from hot water and a bone, and dandelions were free in any empty lot.

"What's the job?"

"A stone smokehouse, up in the mountains."

"Can you handle it?"

He chortled at the foolishness of such a question. "When I was fourteen I built a well in the mountains of Abruzzi. Down through solid rock. Thirty feet deep and ten feet wide. Cold spring water. I did it myself. Carried rock out of the hole, then carried it back. I worked in water up to my ass. It took me three months. I got paid a hundred lira. You know how much that was, in those days? Forty-five cents. Fifteen-cents-a-month wages. Now I got a chance to make fifteen hundred dollars in one month, and you want to know if I can handle it!" This amused him. He laughed. "Of course I can handle it! All I need is a little help."

"Papa, you're a liar. Nobody works for fifteen cents a month."

His fist banged the table.

"I did. And I'll tell you something else. I put away half my wages."

"What'd you do with the other half?"

"Squandered it. Gambled. Got drunk. Slept with some woman."

He quaffed a couple of large mouthfuls of the Musso claret as I studied him. There was no questioning the man's years, especially the eyes. Their sparkle was gone, as if behind a yellowish film and a net of small red veins.

I said, "Papa, I don't think you should take that job."

"Who says so?"

"You're too damned old. You'll have a stroke, or a heart attack. It'll finish you off."

"My mother was ninety-four. My father was eighty-one. All I need is a first-class helper, somebody who knows how to mix mortar and carry stone."

"You got anybody in mind?"

He sipped the claret. "Yep."

"Is he reliable?"

"Hell no, but you take what you can get."

I realized whom he had in mind.

"Papa," I smiled. "You're out of your tree."

"How long can you stay?"

"A day or two."

"We can do it in three weeks."

"Impossible."

"Easy job. Little stone house up at Monte Casino. Ten by ten. No windows. One door. I'll lay up the walls, you mix the mortar, carry the stone. Nice place. Good country. Forest. Big trees. Mountain air. Do you good. Get the fat off."

"Fat? What fat?"

"Fat. Out of shape. I pay ten dollars a day. Board and room. Seven days a week. We'll be outa there in two weeks if you don't waste time or quit on me. You want the job? You got it. But remember who's boss. I do the thinkin'."

"Papa, I want you to listen carefully to what I am about to say. I want you to stay calm, and I want you to be reasonable. My business, as you know, is writing. Your business is building things. All I know how to do is string one word after another, like beads. All you know is piling one rock on another. I don't know how to lay brick or mix mortar. I don't want to know. I have certain things to do. I have a commitment. A commitment is a contract. There's a man in New York, a publisher, who's paying me to write a book. He is waiting for this book. He has been waiting for over a year. He is losing his patience. He sends me angry letters. He telephones and calls me filthy names. He threatens to sue me. You understand what I'm saying, Papa?"

"I'll tell you one thing about Monte Casino," he said. "You'll feel better. You'll get healthy. What are you worrying about? Did I say anything about not writing? Bring some pencils and paper. Ask Mama: she's got lots of paper in the closet. Write any time you want. Write something about the mountains. Write at night, after work. It's quiet up there. You know the owls? You can hear them. And the coyotes. Peace, quiet, purify the mind. You'll write better."

I groaned. "What about Garcia, your old hod carrier?"

"Dead."

"What about Red Griffin?"

"Dead."

"That black man, Campbell."

"Dying."

"There's got to be somebody alive around here besides me? There's got to be!"

"Gone, all gone."

"What about Zarlingo, or Benedetti, or one of these bums at the card table?"

"They're pretty old. Benedetti is eighty."

A sigh, like a sigh coming out of the centuries, spilled from his wine-moist lips. He seemed to crumble, as if his skeletal bones were falling apart beneath the weight of despair, his chin settling on his chest.

"Nobody wants to work for Nick Molise," he said. "I been

looking for two weeks, but I can't find nobody. Not even my own son." He fought back a sob.

"Good God, Papa, don't start crying on me."

"Ten, twenty generations of stonemasons, and I'm the last, the end of the line, and nobody gives a damn, not even my own flesh and blood."

It was time for reasonableness, for patience and soft words, for restraint, for goodness and charity and filial generosity. I said I was sorry, Papa. I said there were some things I would not ask him to do, and there were other things he should not ask me to do. I said I was not against carrying a hod or laying stone. I said masonry was an honorable profession, the best record of the nobility and aspiration of mankind. I spoke gratefully of the Acropolis, the Pyramids, of Roman aqueducts and the Aztec ruins. Then I began to be annoyed by this irascible, stubborn old man, and my impatience spilled over and the Molise rashness swept through me, the truculence, the bad temper, the frenzy.

"Frankly, old man," I said, "I hate the building profession. I've hated it from the time I was a little kid and you used to come home with mortar splattered all over your shoes and face. I think painters and bricklayers are drunks, and I think plumbers are thieves. I think carpenters are crooks and I think electricians are highway robbers. I don't like flagstone or marble or granite or brick or tile or sand or cement. I don't care if I ever see another stone fireplace or stone wall or stone steps or just plain stones lying on a field, and if you want the truth stripped clean I don't give a shit about stonemasons either." I took a deep breath. "Something else I don't like is mountains and forests and owls and mountain air and coyotes and bears. I never saw a smokehouse in my life and, God willing, I shall never see one, or build one."

The more I shouted and pounded the table the more he drank, and the more he drank the more the tears busted from his eyes. He pulled a polka-dot kerchief from his pocket, blew his nose, and had another gulp of wine. He was pitiful, wretched, embarrassing, revolting, shameless, stupid, gross, ugly and drunk — the worst father a man ever had, so loathesome I spat my beer in the spittoon and got up to leave.

From the back of the saloon came the bellow of a voice, the roar of a bull speaking like a man.

"Just a minute, wise guy. Just who the hell you think you're talking to?"

I turned. The patrons of the Café Roma were glaring at me with cold amorphous eyes, their faces repelled by the presence of an outsider in their midst. Zarlingo got to his feet. The many pens and pencils in his bib were like battle decorations on a colonel.

"That man's your father," Zarlingo declared, pointing at Papa. "And he's my friend. You show some respect, understand?"

"It's none of your business."

Cavallaro stood up threateningly, pushing back his chair. "You want some help, Nick? You want me to take care of this punk?"

"I'm okay," Papa faltered, his voice trembling. "I'm just fine, boys. Tired, that's all. Very tired. Alone in the world. Trying to do the right thing. You do your best for your family. You feed them, buy them clothes, send them to school, and then they turn around and throw you out. I don't know what happened . . . what I done wrong. Maybe 'cause I was too good. I don't know. God help me. I tried. I tried hard . . ."

I said "Oh, balls!" and walked out.

7

HALF A BLOCK from my parents' house on Pleasant Street I
breathed the aroma of Mama's cooking. The ugly scene at the
Café Roma vanished in the ambrosial waft of sweet basil,
oregano, rosemary and thyme.

Suddenly a figure burst from the front door of the house,
dashed down the porch steps, and raced to a pickup at the curb.

"Mario!" I shouted. "Mario, wait!"

He either heard me or he didn't hear me as he started the
engine and gunned the noisy truck away without looking at me. I
crossed the yard to the porch. My mother stood behind the screen
door, her silver hair in a neat pile, her apron fresh and white, her
face warmed by happiness and a hot stove. By now Mario's truck
was two blocks away and still farting on five cylinders.

"What's he running from?"

"He ate and ran. Ascared of your father."

"He still eats here?"

"When he can. His wife don't cook Italian." She glanced down
Pleasant Street. "Where's your father?"

"At the Roma."

"You had a fight?"

"Argument."

"You're not going to the mountains?" There was concern in her voice.

"You knew about that?"

We were still talking through the screen door.

"He said he was going to ask you."

"He asked. I said, no chance."

I stepped into the hot, small parlor that was overpowered by the spices from the kitchen. That parlor! It was hellishly hot. A morgue. Walls bedecked with pictures of the dead, aunts, uncles, cousins, grandparents. In the corner on a pedestal stood a statue of Jesus bleeding profusely. Vigil candles in glass cups were at the Savior's feet. They were a vital part of the household, participating in all that was vital and meaningful, for my mother lit the candles whenever a relative died, or when someone got sick, or when something of value was lost, or when lightning came close to the sky.

Dimly I saw a stack of clothing on the sofa. The stuff looked familiar, like images in an old photograph.

"What's all this?"

"Your work clothes."

"*Work* clothes? What kind of work?"

"Mountain work." She hid her face.

"No mountains for me."

"Think about it. Make up your own mind."

"No mountains."

I studied the clothes, tumbled the garments about. God knew where she had dug them out, some trunk in the hot, stuffy attic where everything eventually mummified — jeans, shirts, a pair of boots, even my baseball sweater with the big SE emblazoned on the chest. The idea that even my baby clothes might be carefully preserved somewhere made me shudder. There was something artful about those resurrected garments, a planned arrangement, a spider setting a trap, and I the victim. She sensed my thought and slipped into the kitchen. I found her at the stove, stirring things inside pots. She had prepared a great deal of food.

"Who's going to eat all this?"

"Everybody."

"You invited everybody."

"No, but they'll come anyway."

I dropped into a chair at the kitchen table. She was there right away with a bottle of wine from the refrigerator and a chilled glass. I knew the wine. It had to be the new wine from the vines of Angelo Musso's vineyard, easily the most important commodity in the house, for without it my father would quickly dry up and fade away.

"Mama, what's this about a divorce?"

"What divorce?"

"You know what divorce. Why do you think I'm here?"

She laughed. "Just talk. We're Catholics, we can't divorce. Didn't you know that?"

"Mario said he kicked you, choked you. You had to have him arrested."

"Mario did it. Papa didn't mean it. He didn't do it on purpose."

She began slicing bread.

"How can he kick you, choke you, but not on purpose?"

"He didn't mean it. He was only playing."

"So he went to jail."

"For a half hour. It was nothing."

"What about the lipstick on his underwear?"

"It was jelly."

"I thought it was jelly."

"Cherry jelly. On his pancakes. He spilled some on his lap."

"And for that you accuse him of infidelity?"

"So I was wrong, for once." She heaved a big sigh. "How many times have I been right the last fifty years?"

I took her hand and smoothed the dry, soft skin.

"You don't have to worry about things like that anymore. He's not young anymore. The fire's out."

"He don't need a fire. He keeps going without it."

"In his mind, that's all."

"It's dirty," she said. "It's a sin."

She busied herself with the dinner, checking the eggplant in the oven, the gnocchi warming in a black iron pot, the veal bubbling in Marsala.

"I couldn't find any heavy socks. You'll need them up there. It may snow, this time of the year."

"I'm not going 'up there.' "

"Not even this last time, for your father?"

"I'm working. I can't leave my book."

That sent her suddenly out of the room toward the bedroom, where I heard her shuffling heavy objects about. She returned with an armful of books, dropping them on the table in front of me. They were my high school textbooks: geometry, American history, English composition, Spanish.

"Take them home," she said. "They're still new."

I thanked her. "Just what I need."

She studied my face, her fingers touching the delicate bones of her cheeks as she returned to the one obsession of her existence. "You didn't get him mad? He won't get into trouble?"

"He'll drink too much, that's all."

"I don't mind the drinking. The boys bring him home."

"The boys?"

"Zarlingo and them. They watch him for me. Thank God you'll be there. They scare me, those mountains."

An angel, a persistent, tiresome angel. No wonder my papa booted her in the ass. I felt strangled, helpless as an infant swaddled and straining in futility. What the hell was I doing here? What was my wife up to? I was having a serious problem with my book. What the hell was it? Had the old man really put up with this crap for half a century? Who said he was impulsive, lacking patience, intolerant? The sun had dropped below the houses beyond the alley and it was cooler now, about ninety-five in the shade, the sky exploding with red and orange clouds.

"As long as I know where he is," she was saying. "As long as he lets me know . . ."

I filled my glass and went out on the front porch, sat in the creaking rocker, and lit a cigarette. Darkness came fast. Down the street a mother stepped out on her porch and called her children to supper. The corner street lamp burst into light and an old dog trotted under it, hurrying home. The white eyes of television sets shone through the windows across the street, cowboys racing across the screens, gunfire crackling in the San Elmo twilight. A lonesome town. All the valley towns were like it, desolate, mystically impermanent, enclaves of human existence, people clustered behind small fences and flimsy stucco walls, barricaded against the darkness, waiting. I rocked back and forth and felt grief seeping into my bones, grief for man and the pain of loneliness in the house of my mother and father, aging, waiting, marking time.

Then my mother came quietly to the screen door and stared at me, as if storing up a remembrance of me, as if she might never see me again. I felt her pulsing back and forth, incorporeal and disembodied, sorrowing and lost as she slipped out of reality and back again, ashamed so little time remained.

"Henry?" Her voice was soft and irresolute. "You mustn't worry about me and your father. You get a little crazy when you're older, but it don't do any harm. Be patient, Henry. You want your supper now?"

The baked eggplant took me back to the childhood of my life when they were a nickel apiece and a great feast, purple globular marvels bulging jolly and generous, rich Arab uncles eager to fill our stomachs, so beautiful I wanted to cry.

The thin slices of veal had me fighting tears again as I washed them down with Joe Musso's magnificent wine from the nearby foothills. And the gnocchi prepared in butter and milk finally did it. I covered my eyes over the plate and wept with joy, sopping my tears with a napkin, gurgling as if in my mother's womb, so sweet and peaceful and filling my mouth with life forever. She saw my wet eyes, for there was no hiding them.

"Something in the air," I said. "Ammonia, maybe? It burns my eyes."

"It's ammonia. I mopped the floor with it."

"That's it. Ammonia."

"Your father hates ammonia. He won't let me use it in the washing machine."

"Really?"

"You know what he likes?"

"Tell me."

"Bubble bath."

She veered to questions about Harriet and my boys. I showed her the snapshots in my wallet, the younger twenty-two, the older twenty-four. She studied the pictures under the kitchen light.

"They don't look like stonemasons."

"No."

"Mario's boys don't care for it either. Virgil's boy wants to play the piano and Stella has all girls. He wants a stonemason so bad, poor man. If we had just one in the family I think he'd quit drinking. All his prayers would be answered."

"He prays?"

"Never. Or goes to mass." Her eyes fixed me searchingly. "Do you go to mass, Henry?"

I had anticipated it. "Every Sunday. Like clockwork."

"And your boys?"

"In the same pew with me and their mother, every Sunday."

She almost sailed through the ceiling straight for celestial bliss, but she suddenly caught herself, her face growing serious. "You're lying, Henry. Your wife never turned Catholic."

"I'm working on it. Takes time."

She sat down, sighing, disappointed, pouring a bit of wine into a glass. "No Catholics. No stonemasons. Dear God, whatever happened?"

She reached for my hand and folded it within her dry, warm palms, her voice compassionate and imploring. "Talk to your father, Henry. Make him go back to Our Lord. There isn't much time. When you're his age you never know from one hour to the next. And what'll I do when he goes, worrying about where he went?"

"Why don't you ask Father Martin to talk to him. That's his business, saving souls."

"He's been here lots of times. All they do is fight. Your father has no respect. It's the old country style. He laughs."

"Then leave him alone."

"I hope he goes first. Nobody can put up with him but me. Worse than a child: iron the sheets but not the pillow cases. Starch the cuffs but not the collars. Shine his shoes, trim his mustache, rub his feet, cut his hair, hot water bottle in his bed. You know what he's got now? A bell, by his bed. Every night it rings for something: bring me a glass of wine, rub my back, make me some soup. When I'm gone you think Stella'll do all that?"

The bell puzzled me.

"Don't you sleep together?"

"He threw me out."

"Why?"

"How should I know? I wouldn't touch him anyway." She raced ahead: "Do you know he takes enemas with warm wine, and eats raw eggs in the morning?"

"Nauseating."

"See what I mean?"

A horn sounded from the street.

"That's Virgil. Tell him about the gnocchi."

I walked out on the porch and saw my brother Virgil sitting in his station wagon under the street lamp. I waved him to come in and he motioned me toward the car.

His old wagon was fender-dented, the wood paneling scraped and peeling. We shook hands through the window. We were more like classmates than brothers. Neither of us liked to think of the other, and in that sense we were nonexistent to one another. But he envied me, my lifestyle, my small success that had taken me away from San Elmo. I wasn't sure he hated me, but I was certain he disliked me.

He was porcine now, his navel packed tight against the steering wheel. At forty-seven he looked ten years older, his hair fast vanishing — full at the temples, bald and glistening over the top. He had not married until thirty-five and now he was the father of four girls and a boy. I could smell them as I thrust my head inside the car, the sour taint of vomit and diapers. All the symbols of family joy were piled helter-skelter in the back of the wagon — playpen, tricycles, toys, diapers, blankets.

My brother Virgil! The genius of the family, destined to be a millionaire, straight out of high school with scholastic awards, honored by the faculty and immediately accepted as a clerk in San Elmo's only independent bank. After nearly thirty years with the same firm he now managed the Loan Department, and the future was dim indeed, for the president's three sons, Stanford-educated, had come upon the scene. I felt pity for the guy, but at the same time I thanked God all that baby litter in the back of his car was long gone from my own life.

"How's everything?"

He smiled in a way that bent his mouth out of shape, a man with toothache of the soul. My mother's melancholy eyes took up most of his large Neapolitan face.

"How's Edith?"

"Three guesses." He smiled feebly, like a man on the gallows.

"Good God, Virgil. Not again!"

He nodded with a great head that wearied his shoulders.

"You should stop, Virgil. You ever hear of a drugstore? Use something."

"I use my cock. You have any other suggestions?"

"What about vasectomy?"

"That's for dogs. I'm a man . . . I think."

"Come on in. Let's have a glass of vino."

"I won't go in there," he scowled. "I'm pissed off at them."

"At Mama? Nobody else is here."

"Mama, Papa, Mario, the whole family. That paranoia in front of the police station. I can't take it anymore. They've destroyed me in this fucking town. Now they're trying to bury me."

I opened the door.

"Come on, Virgil. Mama's fixed a lovely dinner."

"Naturally," he smiled. "Tell me something. How come crazy old ladies cook so well? Same thing with my wife's mother. A real psychopath, but God, what stroganoff!" He looked toward the house, tempted, but suddenly he leaned over and jerked the door shut.

"I won't go in there. I'll starve first!"

The screen door squealed and we looked toward the house as Mama stepped outside. "Come and eat, Virgil. It's all fixed."

"No, thanks, Ma."

"Baked eggplant, Virgil," she coaxed. "I fixed it special the way you like it. And gnocchi in milk and butter, and veal in wine."

"Thank you just the same, Ma."

She was hurt and startled by his refusal and slipped back into the darkness of the house. I stared at him.

"Nice going, you jerk."

"I have my reasons."

"How does she know your reasons? All she's thinking about is your gut."

"What's this new madness? Mario says you're going to work for the old man."

"He's crazy."

"I know that. But is it true?"

"Of course it's not true. What kind of an idiot do you take me for? I'm leaving tomorrow morning."

"Leave town, Henry. Leave before they trap you."

"Nobody traps me. I'm my own man."

"Henry," he smiled patiently. "Please. I've heard all that bullshit before. Get out of here as fast as you can. Tonight. Leave now. I'll drive you to the airport."

"Thanks, Virgil. I'm staying."

"The old man's too old to lay stone. Tell him. Then get the hell out."

"If he wants to lay stone, let him. It's his life."

"And it could be the end of his life."

"You want to talk to him, Virgil? You want to reason with that old bastard? He's down at the Café Roma right now. Go on down there and talk it over."

He threw up his hands.

"God, what a family!"

He started the car and I stepped away and watched it move forward about thirty feet. Then it rolled back to where I stood. A foolish, helpless smile crinkled Virgil's fat face.

"Is the eggplant made with bread crumbs and Romano cheese?"

"It sure is."

Resigned, he turned off the engine. Together we walked into the house.

The kitchen. La cucina, the true mother country, this warm cave of the good witch deep in the desolate land of loneliness, with pots of sweet potions bubbling over the fire, a cavern of magic herbs, rosemary and thyme and sage and oregano, balm of lotus that brought sanity to lunatics, peace to the troubled, joy to the joyless, this small twenty-by-twenty world, the altar a kitchen range, the magic circle a checkered tablecloth where the children fed, the old children, lured back to their beginnings, the taste of mother's milk still haunting their memories, fragrance in the nostrils, eyes brightening, the wicked world receding as the old mother witch sheltered her brood from the wolves outside.

Beguiled and voracious Virgil filled his cheeks with gnocchi and eggplant and veal, and flooded them down his gullet with the fabulous grape of Joe Musso, spellbound, captivated, mooning over his great mother, enrapturing her with loving glances, even pausing midst his greed to lift her hand and kiss it gratefully. She laughed to see how completely she had woven her spell, and while they stared like haunted lovers I slipped into the parlor and telephoned Harriet in Redondo Beach.

"Is everything all right up there?" she asked.

"Fine, fine. No problems."

"What about the divorce?"

"Forgotten."

"Did you see my mother?"

"No."

"Will you?"

"Maybe tomorrow."

"Promise?"

"No."

I felt my mother's warm breath on my neck and turned to face her, eavesdropping behind me. Not surreptitiously, but brazenly listening.

"Let me talk," she said, drawing the phone from my hand. Then, into it: "Halloo, Harrietta. She'sa me talkin', you modder-in-law. How you are, Harrietta. Thassa good. Me? I'ma feela fine."

There it was again, my mother's hypocritical fawning before Harriet, that groveling like a serf before the baroness, so self-debasing that even her powers of speech fell apart. Born in Chicago, knowing only the English language, my mother nonetheless spoke like a Neapolitan immigrant fresh off the boat whenever she and Harriet came together.

I listened, exasperated, tearing my hair. "Harrietta, I'ma gonna aska yo wan beeg favor, si? You tink she'sa all right iffen your husba stay two, three day, maybe wan week? He'sa help his papa, poor ole man, he'sa got the rheumatiz. I tink wan week, maybe ten day, maybe two, tree week, and the job, she'sa finish.

Okay, Miss Harrietta? Tank you so much. Godda bless . . ."

I ripped the phone from her. "Home tomorrow, Harriet. Forget all that garbage!"

Mama shoved her mouth into the instrument.

"Please, Harrietta, I hope I donna make trouble in you house, okay? I'm joost try to help his papa. He'sa gotta sore back."

"Home tomorrow!" I yelled, clapping down the receiver.

A clatter of heavy shoes on the front porch, the clumsy movement of bodies. Joe Zarlingo and Lou Cavallaro lurched through the front door carrying my father between them. With calm professionalism, like a nurse, my mother cleared the sofa and fluffed a pillow as the men stretched my father out. He lay there besotted, a smile on his dribbling lips.

"He's smashed," I said, looking down at him.

"I'll get the coffee," Mama said.

Zarlingo and Cavallaro glared at me.

"What brought this on?" I asked.

Zarlingo was shocked. "You got the guts to ask?"

It sickened Cavallaro. "Jesus, man. You ain't even human."

Virgil came from the kitchen, wiping his mouth with a napkin and studying the old man without emotion. Then he moved to the front door, tossed the napkin into a chair, and smiled at me.

"What did I tell you?"

He went through the front door. I stepped out on the front porch and watched him drive away. Another car, a Datsun camper, was parked out there. It was Zarlingo's.

He came from the house with Lou Cavallaro and the two stood silently on either side of me. Zarlingo bit off the tip of a Toscanelli and jabbed it between his teeth.

"You going up to Donner Pass with your father?" he demanded.

"Nope."

"You mean, you want your old man to go up there, haul rock, mix mortar, and build a stone house all by himself?"

"If that's what he wants, I certainly won't stand in his way."

"In other words, you don't give a fuck if your father lives or dies."

"I didn't say that, you did."

"He's a proud man," Cavallaro said. "Don't you understand that by now?"

"Pride goeth before the fall."

Suddenly old Zarlingo hauled off and hit me a loud whack across the cheek with his open palm. It was a stinging smack, surprising, shocking. He seemed more surprised than I at what he had done, and Cavallaro stood there bewildered. I laughed. There was nothing else I could do. I laughed to hide my anger and walked away, down the path to the sidewalk, where I turned to look back, a bloat of rage bulging inside my ribs.

"You creep!" I yelled. "You senile, pathetic old drunk!"

"You punk!" he screamed, charging down the steps toward me. "You better show a little respect."

I thought of standing my ground, even of belting him, but none of it made sense, especially my anger, and I quickly walked away. Over my shoulder I saw him pick up a beer can from the gutter and throw it at me. The can clattered harmlessly past my feet, and that made me laugh again. I continued down the street toward town. My mind clicked into gear: I was leaving that goddamn town. In three or four hours I would be under the covers in my own bed, four hundred miles away, listening to the sigh of the surf, and all of this bad dream would be forgotten. Straight down Pleasant Street I walked to Lincoln, then right on Lincoln to the bus depot.

In the alley the Sacramento bus was breathing hard as it took on a handful of passengers. I bought a ticket and walked back to the bus, but I did not get aboard. I had lost the power to make a decision. The longer I lingered — the driver waiting, watching me through the door — the more momentous the choice became as fear set in, the fear of delivering a fatal blow to my aged parents, the fear of regretting it the rest of my life. I had to stay. Not from choice but duty. And so I turned away and walked home, searching myself for a burst of Christian exhilaration for having done the right thing, building up my reward in heaven.

The Datsun was gone when I reached the house and so were Zarlingo and Cavallaro. In the bedroom my mother sat beside the old man, who lay undressed beneath a sheet in the hot, small room.

"Where'd you go?" my mother said. "I was so worried."

"About what?"

"You're a writer. This town's no place for you at night."

I thought I heard my father sob and moved closer to him. In his sleep he wept, tears spilling from his closed eyes. She blotted his wet lashes with the hem of the sheet.

"Why is he crying?"

"He's dreaming. He wants his mother."

His mother. Dead sixty years.

I choked up and fled to the kitchen, craving wine. I was into the second glass when Mama appeared.

"I changed the sheets, Henry. You sleep in my bed."

8

I WAS TOO TIRED to care. Like all the rooms in that old house, my mother's bedroom was small. The bed was still warm from the heat of the day as I slipped naked beneath a sheet and down into a cradle in the mattress that measured the contours of my mother's body. It was very black down there when I snapped off the bedside lamp. In the pillow my nostrils drew the sweet, earthy odor of my mother's hair, pulling me back to other times, when I was not yet twenty and sought to run away.

Yes, I got away. I made it when I was not yet twenty. The writers drew me away. London, Dreiser, Sherwood Anderson, Thomas Wolfe, Hemingway, Fitzgerald, Silone, Hamsun, Steinbeck. Trapped and barricaded against the darkness and the loneliness of the valley, I used to sit with library books piled on the kitchen table, desolate, listening to the call of the voices in the books, hungering for other towns.

I had come to the limits of shooting pool, playing poker and bullshitting over beers, of driving off with other guys and broads into lonely orchards, clawing clumsily at skirts and panties, clawing in vain. Women were fine but demanding, you hurt easily at nineteen; you thought women were sweet and submissive but find them alley cats; you find comfort in whores who are less deceitful, and if you are lucky you learn to read.

My old man, the son of a bitch, lurching home with a snoutful of vino, yelling turn off the lights, get to bed, what the hell's come over you, for books were a drug and my addiction was alarming, and I was hardly his son at all anymore. Get a job, he demanded, do something with your life. He was right. He must have been. Everybody agreed with him. Even the guys at the poolhall noticed the change. We couldn't talk to one another the old way.

I got a job. I picked almonds. I picked grapes. I worked the hop fields. The rains came, the fields wet and unworkable, thank God, and I was back in the kitchen, reading the sweet books. They thought I was ill — my eyes red and staring, my mother feeling my forehead: You all right, Henry? Maybe you got the flu.

He should see a doctor, my father said. Find out what's wrong. Where you going with your life? Who's gonna take care of your mother when I'm gone? They don't pay wages for reading books. Get out of here! There's a war on. Get in the army. Go to San Francisco. Get on a boat. Support yourself. Be a man. You know what a man is? A man works. He sweats. He digs. He pounds. He builds. He gets a few dollars and puts them away. Listen to who's talking! I sneered.

There was no answer for that street-corner Dago, that low-born Abruzzian wop, the yahoo peasant ginzo, that shit-kicker, that curb crawler. What did *he* know? What had *he* read?

For I was okay. I was on to something. A new feeling of the world beyond San Elmo and television, thrilling, shocking, pumping my adrenalin. Why had I not come upon it before? Where had I been all those years? Trying to carry a hod, mixing mortar? Who was it that had stunted my brain, kept books out of my range, ignored them, despised them? My old man. His ignorance, the frenzy of living under his roof, his rantings, his threats, his greed, his bullying, his gambling. Christmas without money. Graduation a suit of clothes. Debts, debts. We stopped speaking. One day we passed one another crossing the railroad tracks. He went on a few steps, stopped, and began to laugh. I turned. He pointed at me and began to laugh. He pretended to read a book and laughed. It was not amusement. It was rage and disappointment and contempt.

Then it happened. One night as the rain beat on the slanted kitchen roof a great spirit slipped forever into my life. I held his book in my hands and trembled as he spoke to me of man and the world, of love and wisdom, pain and guilt, and I knew I would never be the same. His name was Fyodor Mikhailovich Dostoyevsky. He knew more of fathers and sons than any man in the world, and of brothers and sisters, priests and rogues, guilt and innocence. Dostoyevsky changed me. *The Idiot, The Possessed, The Brothers Karamazov, The Gambler.* He turned me inside out. I found I could breathe, could see invisible horizons. The hatred for my father melted. I loved my father, poor, suffering, haunted wretch. I loved my mother too, and all my family. It was time to become a man, to leave San Elmo and go out into the world. I wanted to think and feel like Dostoyevsky. I wanted to write.

The week before I left town the draft board summoned me to Sacramento for my physical. I was glad to go. Someone other than myself could make my decisions. The army turned me down. I had asthma. Inflammation of the bronchial tubes.

"That's nothing. I've always had it."

"See your doctor."

I got the needed information from a medical book at the public library. Was asthma fatal? It could be. And so be it. Dostoyevsky had epilepsy, I had asthma. To write well a man must have a fatal ailment. It was the only way to deal with the presence of death.

9

MY FIRST DAY in Los Angeles I took a job washing dishes at Clifton's Cafeteria. After a few days I was promoted to busboy and was sacked for "socializing with the public," in this case a girl carrying a volume of Edna St. Vincent Millay who invited me to her table for coffee and a talk on poetry.

Next day I found another dishwashing job at a saloon on the corner of Fifth and Main. My room was upstairs for four dollars a week, shared by another dishwasher. His name was Hernandez and he was crazy. He was the first writer I ever met, a tall, laughing Mexican sitting on the bed with a typewriter in his lap, guffawing at every line he wrote. His project was a book called *Fun and Profit in Dishwashing*. It was as mad as Hernandez himself. I used to fall asleep listening to him read the manuscript, convulsing with pleasure. One of his chapters was "The Mystery of Hot Water," another, "Clean Hands Make Clean Minds."

But the job was exhausting, the floor always submerged from leaking pipes, and the food inedible. I quit to work in the garment district pushing dress racks and running errands for everyone. I had a dozen bosses who kept me rushing after coffee, sandwiches, newspapers and a hundred other trifles. One of them owned an independent cab service and offered me a job driving at night. I accepted though I knew nothing of the huge, complicated city. For eight hours I cruised downtown Los Angeles that first night without catching a single fare. My boss assured me that things would improve when the dry spell ended, and to pray for rain.

The following night I had my first customers, a black man and his girl. The man asked to be driven to Ninety-sixth and Central Avenue. As I consulted a map of the city he said, "You mean to tell me you don't know where Ninety-sixth and Central is?" I told him I was new in town. "I'll show you the way," he said. "Down one block and turn left."

For two hours I followed his directions, all the way to San Bernardino, where I was told to stop in a tractless, houseless wasteland without street lights or sidewalks. I felt the barrel of a pistol in my ear as he ordered me out of the car. His girlfriend searched me and took all I possessed, nine dollars. They drove off, leaving me there in a place resembling Death Valley.

As daylight pulsed in the east, a police car came up silently and found me walking toward what appeared to be the lights of a distant city. I spent three hours in the San Bernardino Police Station being grilled mercilessly by two detectives who suspected me of being AWOL or draft-dodging. The 4-F status of my draft card did not impress them. They fingerprinted me and ran a check. At noon they released me, without breakfast or even coffee, and ordered me out of town. They were bad guys: they wouldn't even give me directions.

I got out on the street and began to ask passers-by. Nobody seemed to know how to get out of San Bernardino, so I finally found it myself. I thumbed for an hour before a truck stopped. The driver wasn't going to Los Angeles but to Wilmington. Good enough. Anything was better than San Bernardino. When I told him of being robbed and arrested he laughed. "Lotsa luck," he said as he let me off on Wilmington Boulevard.

Wilmington was paranoid, a seaport town in the midst of war. It did not seem to have been laid out so much as dumped out. Big trucks hogged the streets, roaring through crowded intersections where soldiers, sailors and civilians ignored traffic signals in the middle of honking claxons and cursing drivers. I moved with the flow of people, aimlessly following a surge down Avalon Boulevard. I was tired, dirty and dazed, tumbled like a cork along a street of oil derricks, factories, lumberyards, piles of girders and steel pipe, row upon row of army tanks and trucks, poolhalls, poker palaces, used-car lots, and even an amusement park with a merry-go-round and a Ferris wheel. The laughter of women in bars flooded the streets. Hustlers leaned in doorways, drunks sat on the curb, smiling cops cruised in bemused attention. Where was I? Liverpool? Singapore? Marseilles? I thought of my father, how he would have loved this singular place — the gambling, the bars, the buildings shooting up on every empty piece of land.

Hunger. I smelled the tomato sauce, the pizza coming from an Italian restaurant. I turned the corner and moved down the alley to the rear of the place. As I knocked on the black screen door a cloud of flies whined away and I saw the face of an Italian woman peering out, a plump woman in her forties, round as a meatball. I'll work for something to eat, I said. She was startled, frowning. I'm hungry, I said. She opened the door and pointed to three overloaded garbage cans, motioning me to take them outside. I rolled them out among the ecstatic flies. She worked swiftly at a butcher's table with half a loaf of French bread split down the middle, hollowed out and filled with pastrami and cream cheese. I thanked her and said I was looking for a job. Experienced dishwasher, I said. She opened the door and invited me out. I went away down the alley to a trailer park where a black hose curled like a snake through uncut lawn, and I sat on a trailer hitch eating the sandwich and drinking warm water from the hose.

Down in the harbor a mile away I came to the Toyo Fish Company. There was a sign: WANTED: MACHINE OPERATORS, LABORERS.

Me, laborer. No hod carrier, me. No stonemason. No
bricklayer. I could hear the old man: learn a trade, be something
special. Oh shit, Papa. I'm not twenty yet, give me time.

The man's name was Coletti. Dark, maybe Sicilian. Foreman of
the labor gang. Paisan, I smiled. He didn't like it. I'm looking for a
job. No jobs, he said. But the sign outside said . . . Maybe
tomorrow, he said.

I walked out into the street, heading for town, up Avalon
Boulevard. But where, and why? I found a bus bench. I would call
Virgil collect and ask him to send money. No, he'd tell Mama,
which was okay, but the old man would find out. He'd laugh. I
warned him, he'd say, he wouldn't listen to his father.

I rose and walked again, my feet aching. I met another bum
like myself. He wore a long overcoat in that hot late afternoon, the
pockets stuffed with junk.

"Hey, where can I get something to eat?"

"They's lots of restaurants," he said.

"I'm broke."

"So am I."

"Where do you eat?"

"Holy Ghost Mission."

"Where's that?"

"Follow me."

Holy Ghost Mission was on Banning Street between two
pawnshops. It had once been a store. A crowd of thirty men, all as
neatly dressed and clean-shaven as myself, crowded the door.
Some sat on the sidewalk, their backs against the storefront. At
seven o'clock the door opened and Mr. Atwater, a black man, told
us to come inside. There was a podium where Mrs. Atwater
stood, holding a guitar. We took our seats on long benches, were
given hymnbooks, and Mrs. Atwater led us in songs. Then Mr.
Atwater stood before us and talked about the mercy of God, the
importance of faith, and the evils of drink. He was a big, soft-
voiced man with a short white beard, a good and gentle man.

After the sermon we were led behind a partition to the dining area, long tables and benches, and two black ladies served us large bowls of beef stew, a hunk of bread and an apple. Everything was free, and it happened every night at seven o'clock. I sighed with relief. I had it made.

That night I slept in a used-car lot on Avalon, an old Cadillac with a velour back seat, comfortable and long enough. At eight o'clock the next morning I was back at the Toyo Fish Company standing in front of Mr. Coletti's desk. He looked up from some papers.

"Nothing today," he said.

"Tomorrow?"

"You never know."

I felt encouraged. I liked Coletti. We were on talking terms, getting acquainted. Every morning I left my Cadillac and trudged down to Toyo for a brief conversation with him. There were never harsh words. Sometimes he glanced at my clothes, the gray suit I had worn since my first day in Los Angeles, rumpled now and soiled and misshapen. "Nothing doing today," he'd say. "Things are still slow." Then one day he let me in on a production matter. "No fish," he said. "We're waiting for the boats." I felt cheered. I had been given confidential information. The job was coming. I had to hold out. Now I need not look for other jobs. God knew I had tried.

Why had I been rejected? Was it my clothes? Was it my face? I studied it in store windows, the dark stubble beard, the gauntness, the aspect of defeat. Did I repel people? Did I give off some mysterious antagonism, some anger at the world? A time came when I became afraid to approach bosses and employers. Only Coletti and Mr. Atwater accepted me, gave me hope and food. I walked the streets. I found the public library and read for hours, then dropped down to the Holy Ghost Mission for my supper. I thought of begging, for I had seen panhandlers scrounging coins and it looked easy. But I lacked courage. I was too ashamed. Even those heady days when I made my way in Los Angeles washing dishes seemed impossible now.

After a month in Wilmington, Coletti came through. "You start tomorrow. Be here at seven."

I wanted to kiss his hand, but I only said, "Thank you."

I walked away with my chest bursting in joy and pain, past the docks where stevedores loaded ships and men steered forklifts, laughing and kidding as they worked, and I laughed too, for I was one of them, I had a job, I belonged to the human race again. At the Holy Ghost Mission I sang with a full throat, and I cried when Mr. Atwater spoke of the mercy of God. When they passed out the gleaming red Washington apples I held mine like a holy goblet, too sacred to devour.

An old lady with a few teeth like fangs sat next to me. I smiled and said, "Would you like another apple?" She nodded with a smile and accepted my apple and put it in her paper sack. I felt ennobled. I had given something instead of taking.

It was time to sleep now, to retire and prepare for my first day on the job. As I entered my Cadillac and stretched out, the used-car manager pounced on me and ordered me out of the car. He raised a jackhandle as if to smash my skull. "Get the fuck outa here, you bum. Next time I'll call the cops."

When you are a drifter you take note of places to bed down — abandoned buildings, open basements, sheds. I had such a place filed away in my mind — a hideaway beneath a bridge over the Tucker River, which wasn't a river at all except when it rained.

On the way to Tucker Bridge I stopped at the Catalina Steamship Terminal to pick up some cigarettes. The terminal was without doubt the best source of cigarettes in the harbor. It supplied the top brands — Pall Mall, Tareyton and Chesterfield — in king sizes and in ample quantities. This was the best hour to go there and stock up, for the *Catalina* had just returned from the island and the passengers had departed. I was not disappointed. Every sand-filled ashtray was crammed with lovely butts, and I went from one to another, selecting my favorite brands and stuffing them into my coat pockets. It had been a good day for me.

The new job, an excellent meal at Holy Ghost, and enough cigarettes to get through the following day.

A butter moon lit the harbor as I trudged through weeds and sand to the entrance of Tucker Bridge. The stream was no more than a trickle of sewer water through white sand. Someone had dragged a skiff beneath the bridge and covered it with a tarp. I rolled the canvas up and shaped it into a mattress. How beautiful it was under that bridge! Yellow moonbeams flooded both openings, and the water laughed as the tide splashed the pilings with its ebb and flow.

I lay on my back and thought of the future. Any hopes for writing would have to be postponed. What mattered now was just staying alive. From that day forward I resolved never to be poor again. I would work hard for Coletti and the Toyo Fish Company. I would hoard every penny. I would jingle coins in my pocket and store away dollars in the bank. I would cover my body, my life, with money. I would be impregnable. I would not be hurt again. I was still a young man. On December 8, a month from now, I would be twenty years old. There was plenty of time. I had everything going at last in my favor. I smiled as I said the Lord's Prayer.

Something bit me and I wakened. Something on my leg. I sat up. Something stung my hand, the small finger. I flicked my hand. I looked. A beast, an animal, a thing, clinging to my finger. It was a brown thing. It was a crab. It hung on. I beat it against the boat. It fell away. I sat up. They were all over me. They were on my legs, under my pants, they were biting, crawling. I felt them at my scrotum. I pulled one out of my hair. I jumped up and screamed. They fell from my clothes. They made a sound of clicking. I jumped up and down. I screamed in fear. I ran out from under the bridge and tore off my clothes in the daylight. I saw the traffic. I pulled off my pants, my shirt, my shorts. I was naked, on fire, rubbing sand into little bleeding holes in my body, running like crazy, flinging myself in weeds and sand, howling like a dog.

I heard a siren. I saw the spinning red light. I saw the police car roaring down, churning up sand. Two cops with batons rushed at me. "My clothes!" I said, grabbing at them — a shirt, my coat, my pants — the cops scrambling after me as I crawled on hands and knees. They picked me up by the armpits and staggered toward the police car. They opened the door and tossed me inside, the clothes in my arms. I covered my groin with the clothes and began to shake out of control as the car roared away and my teeth chattered as I kept dying and trying to stay alive.

They took me to the emergency room of the hospital, slamming to a stop in the driveway.

"Put your pants on," the older cop said.

I fumbled with the bundle of sand-laden clothes, teeth clicking, hands shaking the loose sand on the seat and the carpet. The old cop was furious. "Watch it with that sand!" He unfolded a blanket and opened the door. He threw the blanket over me as I got out.

They marched me into the side door of the emergency room and the old cop snatched away the blanket. He threw it on the floor in disgust. The medic stared as I stood clutching my clothes.

"Got a beauty this time, Doc." the old cop smiled.

The medic was a blond guy of about thirty in a blue smock. A fingernail gently scraped the flesh at my shoulder. The dirty skin was as greenish gray as a mackerel.

"You ever had a bath before?" the medic asked.

"I used to bathe all the time."

"Put your clothes on the chair and follow me."

I spilled my rags on the chair and went down the hall with him to a shower. He handed me a bar of soap and a towel. I got under the hot water. It was as close to heaven as I had ever been. It stopped the shaking and I began to see the pink of my flesh. I toweled off and walked back to the emergency room. The cops were still there, smoking and talking to the doctor. I lay on the table and he dabbed the wounds with a yellowish antiseptic as the old cop began to question me: name, address, draft status. Quietly he asked, "How long you been doing this?"

I looked at him. "Doing what?"

"Indecent exposure."

I sat up.

"Never!"

I was shaking again as I told about the crab attack. They were amused but not convinced. I thrust out my arms, my legs, to show the gouged flesh. The cops were not impressed.

"Could be self-inflicted," the old cop said, turning to the doctor. "What do you think, Doc?"

My gut hardened and my eyes devoured the medic. He had been rather friendly and dispassionate, a professional but not a cop. I screamed at him.

"Tell them!"

He looked from me to the two cops, then turned back to swabbing the wounds. "I don't believe they're self-inflicted," he said. "But I don't think he was attacked by crabs either."

I felt the grief in my chest, the turmoil to break into tears. God almighty, don't make me cry. God keep me a man like my father!

Suddenly the old cop jumped away.

"Jesus Christ!" he said, looking down at the floor. Crawling toward him, skittering across the gleaming tile floor, was a crab. Another was moving frantically toward the crack in the door. A third crawled out of the leg of my pants, his feelers moving as he checked the strange territory. I cried then. I sat up and held my knees and cried because everybody was so fucking rotten, and the only ones coming to my rescue were the little beasties who had caused all the trouble in the first place, the crabs.

My outburst chilled the cops. They backed out of the room and returned to the squad car. Through the window I saw them sitting in the front seat, heads back, caps pulled over their eyes.

The medic washed his hands. He looked disturbed as he dried them on a towel. "Let's have a look at those crab bites again," he suggested, murmuring to himself as he probed here and there. "I think I'll give you a tetanus shot," he said. "You ever had one?" I told him yes, a couple of years ago. Turning me over on my stomach, he jabbed a hypodermic into my butt. It hurt and I sat up.

"Is that all?"

"Not quite. I'm giving you penicillin too."

I took it in the arm.

"Okay. You can get dressed."

I picked up my sand-laden pants. They were obscene and disgusting as I held them in the air.

"If the cops don't mind, I'd just as soon have their blanket."

"I'll fix that," the medic said.

He walked down the hall and returned with a pair of Levi's, a gray sweatshirt, shorts and socks. They were old but clean. I thanked him and got dressed as he chased the crabs around with a rag saturated in chloroform.

We said so long and I walked out to the police car and was driven to the Wilmington Substation of the L.A.P.D. I was booked on a charge of vagrancy. They put me in a holding cell with four other criminals, and around noon the police van hauled us to Lincoln Heights Jail in Los Angeles.

I thought of the Toyo Fish Company and all that it had promised, and how beautiful it was, rotting away there on the dock, all tin and stinking enchantingly of fish and bilge and scum and tar, and I thought fondly of Coletti, who believed in me, and I wondered if I was really as old as I felt. I looked at the other prisoners in the van. They had been arrested for brawling — their eyes blackened, some with bandaged heads and knuckles. What a sad bunch we were, riding off in the warm sunshine.

We ended our journey in the drunk tank at Lincoln Heights, an oversized cell where tired, waiting men slumped on wooden benches, shriveled in their clothes.

The next morning fifty of us were marched before the judge in

Sunrise Court. When my name was called I stepped forward and pleaded guilty to the charge of vagrancy. There wasn't much choice. Had I pleaded innocent without the necessary bail, the court would have confined me for two months while I waited for a trial date and the assignment of a public defender. The judge fined me ten dollars or five days.

The fourth morning of my term I woke to see an old acquaintance, brought in during the night. It was Crazy Hernandez, the dishwashing writer, sitting on his bunk smoking a cigarette. He leaped at me like a beloved friend, dancing me around the cell. Hernandez was charged with marijuana possession. Not only was he charged with it, he was actually smoking it, the joint concealed in his cupped hands. That explained his enthusiasm at our reunion. Taking advantage of his euphoria, I asked him to loan me some money.

"All I got!" He pulled off his shoe, dug a bill from inside, and slapped it into my hand. A dollar. "There's more where that came from!" he boasted. It was not so. I saw the inside of the shoe and there was nothing more within.

Oh, that Hernandez! He would never know what his dollar meant to me the morning I was sprung — a ride on the Big Red Car back to the harbor, no hitchhiking, no dread of being snatched again by the cops, a ride back to the Toyo Fish Company and my friend Coletti.

He was studying some papers at his desk.

I said, "Hi, Mr. Coletti."

"I thought you wanted to work."

"I was sick, in the hospital."

"You look sick now."

"I'm okay."

"See Julio in the warehouse."

Julio was the straw boss over the labor crew — ten men, six Mexicans, four Filipinos. They were loading a railroad car with cartons of canned tuna. I pitched in. They tossed those cartons as if they were basketballs, laughing and horsing around. I had to boost each one with the last of my strength. It was a long day, and when it was over I could not close my fingers.

I went back to Coletti's office. He was slipping into his coat. "Well?"

"Could you pay me for today?"

"We don't do that here."

"I have to get a room."

"Jesus, you're a lot of trouble."

But he gave me six dollars from the cash drawer.

10

I WAS A FAILURE at the Toyo Fish Company. A disgrace to myself. I could not pack it. The work was too much for me. At eighteen, in my last year of high school, my weight had been 160 pounds, not a big man but a solid, stumpy man with hard muscles and strong legs, a tough halfback, a swift baseball player. In the cannery it was another kind of game. The wiry Filipinos, the tireless Mexicans, made a counterfeit of me and I was ashamed, lashing myself in futility. They hoisted 100-pound sacks of rock salt with ease while I staggered with a blue face and let them slip from my grasp. They shoveled crushed ice by the hour while I rested, out of breath. My boss, Julio, observed quietly and said nothing. The other men saw it too, and pretended not to see it. They were waiting out the ordeal, waiting for me to throw in the towel. Even Coletti began to appear, watching the work from a doorway, looking a moment and then walking away. A day came when we had to clear tons of ice from the hold of a half-sunk tuna clipper. In hip boots we slushed in ice water for two days. I stopped to rest on a pile of sacks and fell asleep. Julio wakened me. The job had been finished, the ice cleared away. I was cold and shivering. Coletti wanted to see me.

"You're fired," he said, handing me a paycheck.

I had been with the Toyo Fish Company for two weeks and two days. The check was in full payment for the third week.

"A little bonus," Coletti said.

What now? A man who could not even shovel fish fertilizer, where did I fit in the world? I remembered another lifetime, the holy hours with Dostoyevsky, and I knew it could never be that way again. A janitor, maybe? A little tobacco shop? A bellhop? My grandfather, my father's father. He had been an itinerant knife-sharpener in Abruzzi. Was that my destiny too? Suddenly I wanted to go home, to my father's house, to my mother's arms, to her minestrone, to my old bed, to lie there the rest of my life. But it was impossible. How could I face them? I had written a few letters home those first days — all fabrications, all lies. I could never confront them now.

It was good timing. I arrived in San Elmo three hours after the flu hit me. My mother turned from the kitchen sink to find me in the doorway.

"Henry! My God, what happened?"

She put me to bed. She brought hot soup. She called Dr. Maselli. He left antibiotics. I wakened and my father looked down at me.

"How do you feel?"

"Great," I said.

"How long you gonna stay?"

"Long as I can."

"You wanna work for me?"

"Not right this moment."

"Sleep. We'll talk later."

I ate and slept. Sometimes I slept and ate. Then my colon tightened. My mother brought me an enema bag. The potion didn't work. She brought another. I locked the bathroom door and applied it. Success! It roared from me. On the other side of the door my mother applauded. "Thank God, oh, thank God!"

It was as if the purge had burst away all that troubled me — the poisons of the body, the abominations of the soul. In the morning I felt clean and pure. I set up a bridge table by the window and started to write.

I wrote in longhand, on lined paper in a grade school tablet, for of typewriters I knew nothing nor cared. My penmanship sufficed, for neat it was, painstaking and clean. In two days it was done: a short story about the Toyo Fish Company, the boys and girls who worked there, and of a love affair between my boss Jose and a Mexican girl. When it was done I paused to see what I had wrought. No, it was not Fyodor Dostoyevsky. I didn't know what it was. A pastiche. It was Jack London, Raymond Chandler, James M. Cain, Hemingway, Steinbeck and Scott Fitzgerald. It even showed traces of Henry Molise. A marvel, a thing of beauty. What to do with it? Where could I realize the most money? *The Saturday Evening Post,* of course. I sent it off, tablet and all.

It was returned so quickly I wondered if it had ever left town and gone all the way to Philadelphia and back. I smiled at the rejection slip. It didn't matter. I had another story ready to mail. The new one went off to *The Saturday Evening Post,* the other to *Collier's.* In two months — fending off the old man with one hand and writing with the other — I completed five stories about the cannery, about Los Angeles harbor, about Filipinos and Mexicans. Not a word of appreciation from the *Post* or *Collier's.* Not a human written line acknowledging my existence. Minutely I examined every page of the rejected manuscripts. Not so much as a fingerprint or smudge, not a mark. A bad time. The old man watched me as he would an unwanted dog that had to be dealt with, a dog that ate too much and left fur on the sofa. There was a time when he growled because I read too much. Now he snarled because I wrote too much. It came down to that last valiant effort. I finished the story of Crazy Hernandez and rushed it to the *Post.* With it went my last hopes for escaping brick and stone and cement. The story sped back even faster than the others, it seemed, and I sat on the porch steps and tore open the brown envelope. I got a shock. There was a letter affixed to the manuscript. It read:

Dear Mr. Molise:
What have you got against the typewriter? If you will type this manuscript on regular 8 1/2 x 11 inch paper I shall be glad to look at it again. The printer would never touch it in its present form.

Sincerely yours,

I forced myself to walk slowly to the *San Elmo Journal*. There was this exploding heartbeat in my throat, the fear I would drop in the street with the story of Crazy Hernandez clutched in my arms. I handed it to Art Cohen, the *Journal* editor and my high school English instructor. He led me to a typewriter in the rear of the office and sat me before it. For half an hour he instructed me on the operation of a typewriter. Then I was on my own. It had taken me two days to write the Crazy Hernandez story. It took me ten days to type it without errors. What matter, ten days? When the check came I would go to San Francisco and find a room in North Beach. I would buy a typewriter, set it up before a window overlooking the bay, and write. Best of all, I wouldn't have to worry about carrying a hod, mixing mud, and mucking around in wet concrete.

What's that, Dostoyevsky? You don't approve of *The Saturday Evening Post*? Well, let me tell you something, Fyodor. I saw your journalistic pieces of 1875, and frankly, they were pretty tacky and commercial, but they brought you plenty of rubles. So let's not blush at the *Post* story. You have done worse in your time . . .

I lay there in the darkness, in the cradle of my mother's mattress breathing the sweet essence of her hair, and there he was again, my tireless old man, still trying to drag me into those deadly mountains where the concrete waited and some fool wanted a smokehouse built. So it had come down to this. After thirty years I had seen the light. I was a hod carrier at long last.

11

NOISE WAKENED ME in the morning — the shuffle of thick shoes past my window, the tumble of lumber, bellowing voices, laughter. The sun was up, hot and full of mischief as it tried to pierce the blinds.

I found an old flannel robe of my mother's in the closet and walked out on the front porch. Zarlingo, Cavallaro and my father were hauling building materials to the Datsun out front and lifting them into the camper — planks, shovels, mortarboards, a wheelbarrow, tools. They sweated in the morning heat; the back of Papa's khaki shirt was soaked down the spine, his face as red as a rose.

They paused at the truck to wipe their faces and sip beer from cans. The sky was a cloudless sheet of blue fire, tremulous, vast. It was a minute or so before they saw me.

"Ain't you dressed yet?" my father said.

"No, I ain't dressed yet."

"Why don't you get dressed like everybody else?"

"I just woke up. Do you mind?"

"You workin' for me or not?"

"We're not in the mountains yet."

Zarlingo looked inside the camper.

"Oh shit. We're outa beer."

"Let's go down to the Roma," Papa said. "I like that tap beer better." He squinted at me through the burning sunlight. "Put on some clothes. That's your mother's robe. Take it off. We leave in an hour. You be ready."

They climbed into the cab, Zarlingo behind the wheel. I didn't like the look of it. The air was shimmering with diabolic vibrations. As the camper moved off I yelled. Zarlingo braked to a stop and I walked to the car. Nick put his head out the window.

"What's the matter now?"

I nodded at his two friends. "Are these two winos working for you too? If they are, I resign right now."

"Resign?" he exploded. "You ain't even started!"

"Well, are they, or are they not?"

Zarlingo put a placating hand on Papa's knee to defuse him. "Let me talk to the lad, Nick." He turned to me. "Look, sonny. We're not working for your dad."

I said, "Don't call me sonny."

"We're just trying to give him a hand," he went on. "Okay, buster? So why don't you shut up and bug off?"

"Mannaggia!" my father howled, tumbling from the car and facing me nose to nose, splashing me with spit. "What are you tryin' to do to me? These fellas are my friends. They're doin' me a favor, hauling all my stuff to the job free of charge, so what right you got to talk like that? Use your head. Show some respect."

Injured and affronted, Zarlingo and Cavallaro looked straight ahead. I didn't care how Papa defended them, they were mean, malevolent old bastards and it was impossible to be civil to them, but I said it anyway, merely to make peace.

"I'm sorry."

They remained rigid and outraged. My father got back into the cab. "Let's get outa here," he said. Zarlingo shifted gears, and as the car moved off Papa stuck his head out the window.

"Get dressed, goddamnit. And take off that robe."

I shuddered from it, those dreadful vibrations: there was something stupid and inexorable about the whole matter, a trap, a dark hole alive with rattlesnakes. Then and there I should have fled the scene, even in my mother's old flannel robe I should have grabbed the first bus out of town.

Instead I showered and shaved and put on the ancient garments of my youth — corduroys, a sweatshirt, a pair of misshapen hobnail boots. How bizarre it was, the feeling inside those old clothes, a snake shedding his skin only to find an older skin beneath. I felt like an old man of sixteen.

They puzzled my mother. She didn't care for them.

"You look too young," she said.

"They feel crazy."

I wanted to say they felt like the garments of someone who had died, the time of my young manhood, a time of stress and crisis, the family poverty in the midst of my father's prosperity, the rage at him, the conviction that God did not rule the world after all, the hunger to lust and achieve, to jump the fences of home and town, to change myself into somebody else, to write, to fuck and write.

Eating breakfast I sensed a change of perspective growing out of the change of clothing — the same knives and forks of my youth, the same plates, the smooth worn handle of the same bread knife, the aging crucifix hanging above the stove — all things old and smooth and soft as the inside of my mother's hand. She watched as I sipped coffee, her eyes troubled, uncertain of my identity.

"You don't have to work for your father. Maybe you shouldn't."

"I know."

"Do what's right — for yourself."

The morality of it was not the question. What mattered was that I had seen death glowing through the face of an old man clinging fiercely to life. No wonder he was stubborn, capricious, self-serving and touched with madness. But he was still my father. If I turned from him in his last cry for achievement it might bring a swifter death, and I did not want that shadow over the rest of my life. I had never actually refused to go to the mountains with him. I had simply allowed him and my mother to draw me into the plan. My father was entitled to this last paltry triumph, this little house of stone in the Sierras.

12

WITH HALF AN HOUR remaining before we took off, I decided to surprise my wife by visiting her mother. Hilda Dietrich was eighty, living alone in a jewel box of a white house a few blocks away. The house was a hundred years old, quite small, a veranda of white pillars encircling it, honeysuckle and climbing roses scaling the trellised portico. The grounds were so clean and neat they resembled a theatrical set. From the white picket fence in front to the tall eugenia hedge bordering the alley there spread an acre of dicondra lawn surrounding flowerbeds and birdbaths. Not a twig or fallen leaf marred that sweep of grass. Regionally the place was famous. Everyone took pictures of it, a California original, passionately cared for by a proud old lady who had made it her life's work.

Hilda Dietrich and I had one common bond that held us together forever: we loathed each other. She had never forgiven Harriet for becoming my wife, and I had never forgiven her for being my wife's mother.

It was my Italian side that Hilda found unbearable. San Elmo has changed now, but forty years ago the town was one-third

Italian. The bluebloods of the region, the Protestant-Americans — the Schmids, the Eicheldorns, the Kisbergs and the Dietrichs — suddenly found themselves horrified neighbors of noisy Dagos working the tracks of the Southern Pacific. They propagated large and offensively dark families and built a Roman church to administer to their primitive superstitions.

With the coming of Prohibition, many of these guineas moved into the bootleg trade. They bought land, cultivated vineyards, and achieved an annoying respectability despite some bombings and a couple of gang killings. In 1926 the front of the Café Roma was blown out, and in 1931 a hood named Petresini was shot down on the corner of Lincoln and Vernon. The bullets that killed Petresini lodged deeply into a telephone pole at the scene, and every generation of kids thereafter probed the bulletholes like Saint Thomas putting his doubting finger into the Savior's wounds.

By Franklin Roosevelt's time Hilda Dietrich was forty, a housewife and mother, married to the Reverend Herman Dietrich, pastor of the Lutheran church. Like her husband, who said as much from his pulpit, Mrs. Dietrich was fully persuaded that Italians were creatures with African blood, that all Italians carried knives, and that the country was in the clutches of the Mafia. It was no extremist theory. A lot of worried people believed it, particularly Italian-Americans.

I met Harriet Dietrich the year after her father died, in the summer of my first book. She was home from Berkeley, working as an assistant in the public library. I autographed the two library copies and she clutched them to her breast and praised my work, the nobility of purpose, the fresh style, et cetera. I was better than Faulkner, she insisted, better than Hemingway. I agreed and went reeling out of the library, intoxicated. What a lovely mind she had! So well informed, so perceptive, with an overview of world literature that took my breath away. As night fell four hours later I was standing on her front porch, eager to continue our stimulating conversation.

Since I had not been invited, she was surprised to see me, smiling her welcome and opening the door to a small Victorian parlor with red velvet chairs and a love seat. In a whisper she explained that her mother had already gone to bed in the next room. I allowed this to alarm me, and I apologized and made for the front door, knowing she would stop me, which she promptly did, steering me back to the love seat, where I kept looking at her noble, smooth, sensuous bottom and wondering if her pubic hair was as blond as her shoulder-length tresses. Her voice was as soft as the night wind, and I fancied her cherry mouth whispering, "Fuck me, please fuck me, Henry!" I saw her golden knees crossing and uncrossing under a short skirt and sighed at the thought of being trapped between them in a scissor lock. With every breath her bosom lifted and I toyed with the reverie of raising her breasts out of her dress in some dramatic way, as if lifting golden goblets toward the sky. Surely I would ball this woman, for already we were beneath each other's skin, slithering for positions. It was not love, but lust was better.

Then Mrs. Dietrich called from her bedroom, sharply, irritably. "Harriet, will you come here, please?"

Harriet looked threatened, smiling nervously as she excused herself and opened the bedroom door. The room was in darkness. As Harriet closed the door there was a buzz of whispered angry voices. In a moment or two Harriet emerged, eyes blazing with anger. She avoided my glance and calmed herself.

"Something wrong?" I asked.

She smiled. "I hate to ask you this, but are you . . . armed?"

"You mean, carrying a gun?"

It was so absurd that she laughed. "Mother says you — you might have a knife."

"Why?"

"You're Italian."

I said, "Oh, shit, she's crazy."

The bedroom door opened and Mrs. Dietrich stood there in a housecoat over her nightie, her feet in slippers. It was said that she had been one of the town's most beautiful women. Not so, then. She had jowls and the cords in her neck protruded, but her figure was rounded and attractive. Raising her arm imperiously, she pointed to the front door.

"Out!" she demanded. "Out of my house, young man, or I shall call the police."

I glanced at Harriet. "What's this all about?"

"Please go," she said, taking my hand. "Please."

I walked to the door with her. "What's going on here?"

Gently she pushed me out on the porch. "I'll see you tomorrow at the library."

"Close that door," Mrs. Dietrich snapped.

Harriet was brave, but she had been taught to fear her intractable mother. Mrs. Dietrich of course forbade her to ever see me again, so we were forced to go underground. It wasn't easy in Placer County. There were Dietrichs everywhere — in towns, on farms and in mountain settlements. Driving separate cars, we used to meet in roadhouses, on back roads, in abandoned farmhouses, in orchards and vineyards.

If a Dietrich cousin or uncle spotted us, a report was telephoned to the queen in San Elmo. It was sport at first, but after two months we tired of it. One morning in July I pulled up in front of the public library, took Harriet by the arm, and led her down to the car. We drove to the Nevada side of Lake Tahoe and were married by a justice of the peace. We spent our honeymoon at a hotel beside the lake, and the following morning we started back to San Elmo for a confrontation with La Dietrich. It was raining hard as we drew up in front of the Dietrich house.

As we stepped from the car Mrs. Dietrich emerged from the house in a raincoat, carrying an umbrella. Her bleak tight-mouthed glare, the protruding cords in her neck, told us she already knew and that there was nothing to say. Hand in hand we moved up the porch steps. Harriet braved a smile.

"Mother, Henry and I are married."

Mrs. Dietrich raised her umbrella and whacked me over the head. That was twenty-five years ago, and Harriet and her mother had long since made an adjustment to the marriage. They corresponded, talked by telephone, and our two sons spent frequent summers with their grandmother in San Elmo. But Henry Molise was anathema. His name, his books, his films were never discussed in the Dietrich house. Whenever we visited San Elmo, Harriet stayed at her mother's house and I lived with my parents. However, four years ago Hilda Dietrich was laid low by pneumonia and Harriet and I flew up because her doctor said it was critical and advised us to come. It was the first and last time I stayed in the Dietrich house.

I avoided the sick woman as much as possible, playing golf by day, staying out of sight, careful not to agitate her condition. To the doctor's amazement she was well and on her feet two days after we arrived. He called it a miracle of antibiotics, but I knew better. Hilda Dietrich had simply willed herself back to health in order to get me out from under her roof. As we left for home she stepped out on the porch to kiss Harriet good-bye and thank her for coming.

Ignoring my hand, she said, "Good-bye, Mr. Malice."

"Molise," I corrected.

She smiled wickedly. "Oh, what's the difference!"

We descended the stairs to a waiting taxi.

"Bitch," I said.

"Be tolerant," Harriet said.

"Bitch."

I rang Hilda Dietrich's door chimes four times before the curtains parted and the old lady's white face appeared behind the glass door, her cold eyes widening in annoyance. She stood there, staring, making no move to open the door.

I said, "Good morning."

"What is it?" she asked.

"Harriet asked me to drop by."

"What on earth for?"

"Just a visit. To see how you're getting along."

She hesitated. "I'm very busy now. Tell Harriet I'm getting along fine."

"I'll only stay a moment."

"Some other time, Mr. Malice."

"Molise," I pronounced. "With an o."

"As long as you're here, I wish you'd take your golf clubs with you."

I had left the clubs when we visited during her illness. Deliberately, for I liked the local course but not the nuisance of traveling with golf clubs. Besides, I had another set at home.

"I'd rather leave them here, if they're not in the way."

"They most certainly are," she snapped.

"In that case, I'll take them away," I said, expecting her to open the door.

"You'll find them in the toolhouse."

The conversation came to a frozen halt as we stared at one another and I felt the boil of blood in my throat, the urge to take her corded old neck in my two hands and break it.

The depth of her dislike was unfathomable. Harriet had said she was "changed." Was this the change, that she hated me more? What had I done to this woman? Had I been cruel to her daughter, or caught in the sack with another woman, the measure of a mother's bitterness would have been understandable. But there was more than hatred in those aged, glittering eyes. Fear was there, paranoia, a sickening obsession, the dread that I might slash her with a knife, Italian-style. Nothing I said or did would rid it from her mind, and it left me sickened and enraged.

I turned away, quickly descending the porch stairs and hurrying around the house to the toolshed. My golf clubs! I had tucked them out of the way in the far corner of a bedroom closet. My clubs! My beautiful custom-made Stan Thompsons, four woods, nine irons, with special grips, featherlike graphite shafts — expensive, perfectly balanced weapons that fired a ball true and far.

And there they were, on the moist adobe floor of the toolhouse, the leather bag flaking apart as I lifted it. Shocking. A disaster. As sacrilegious as spitting out the sacred host. Only a golfer could comprehend this wanton, brutal crime. Every club was rusted, every grip peeling away from the shaft. It was more than the murder of golf clubs. It was an attack on me, my life, my pleasure. Only a deranged mind could conjure up such a desecration.

I wanted revenge, to strike back, to destroy. I looked around and saw them hanging neatly from hooks — her rakes, shovels, clippers, garden tools. I snatched a saw and a shovel and breathed a gloating sigh as the saw's teeth ripped apart the handle of the shovel. But after it was done I felt absurd and embarrassed.

Then I discovered the gloves, a woman's leather gardening gloves hanging from a nail, shaped like the small hands of Hilda Dietrich. I unzipped my fly and poured the golden liquid into them. They had a human form as I hung them up again: they were filled out, grotesque, seeping, the palms open, moist and supplicating.

13

THE THREE SENIORS were waiting in the Datsun camper when I got back to the house — Zarlingo behind the wheel, my father between him and Cavallaro.

"Where you been?" my father asked thickly, his tongue dragging. "Get a move on."

I strode up and studied their slowing faces. Cavallaro might have been sober, but Zarlingo and my father were drunk, smoking long cigars. Zarlingo was quite gone, drooling from the corners of his mouth.

He said, "Let's get out of here."

"You're too drunk to drive," I said.

He smiled moronically.

"Wassa matter, punk? Scared?"

"Scared to death. I'm not going."

I started toward the house, leaving them staring. My mother watched from behind the screen door. "They're bad company, Henry. Be a good boy. Don't go with them."

She followed me into the kitchen and watched as I made a salami sandwich. "I had an awful dream last night," she remembered. "The car went over a cliff and you were killed. Your chest was broke wide open, and you kept screaming, but nobody came."

"Gee, Ma. Thanks for telling me."

Cavallaro walked through the house and stood hesitantly in the kitchen door.

"What do *you* want?" I said.

"Would you feel any better if I drove?"

"How sober are you?"

"Two beers, so help me God."

I bit into the sandwich and thought it over. Cavallaro was trying to be reasonable. He had none of Zarlingo's boorishness.

"Mama," I said. "Can you trust this man?"

She moved to him and looked up at his face.

"Swear you won't drink, Louie."

"I swear," he said, raising his right hand.

"Swear by the blood of the Blessed Virgin."

"I swear."

Mama gave me a confident smile. "Go with them, Henry. Everything's gonna be all right." Suddenly the camera of my fate projected a dark sea and I saw fish swimming among my white, clean bones. I looked at Cavallaro, at my mother, and I was mystified. Maybe the man who had pissed into the gloves was the maddest of them all.

They wanted me up front with them in the cab, but I stopped that one immediately.

"Lotsa room," Papa said. "Sit on my lap."

"No, thanks, Daddy-O. I'll make out in the camper."

It was heaped with Papa's junk, which I moved this way and that until there was a place to upright the wheelbarrow. I spread a canvas over it and seated myself guru-style. No doubt Zarlingo's wife had hung the pink organdy curtains. The interior was like a mobile whorehouse where a bricklayer with all his paraphernalia was being serviced. Peering through the window, I saw my mother weeping and waving a handkerchief as I gazed mournfully at what might be my last look at the house. Cavallaro cruised down Pleasant Street to Lincoln, then east on Vernon to Highway 80.

A few miles out of town the old tomcats began harmonizing, belting out the immortals of their youth: "Let Me Call You Sweetheart," "The Prisoner's Song," and "Three O'Clock in the Morning." They were horribly out of tune, but they were happy too, companions of the road, free, going places, adventuring into old times.

Through the window the lovely autumn hillsides glided by, the manzanita, the scrub oak and pine, the farmhouses, the vineyards, cattle and sheep grazing among white stones, the peach and pear orchards. Autumn up here was a strong season when the earth showed its muscle and its fertility, and there was a wild feeling in the air.

There was a knock on the window behind the seat. I opened it. "Want a beer?" my father asked.

"Sure."

He passed it through, dripping and cold from the cooler, gorgeous in my warm throat, perfection, with the hot sun above, the white peaks of the Sierras in the distance, and the Datsun humming confidently along the wide highway. I felt good now. Perhaps the trip would turn out well after all.

14

Twenty miles east of San Elmo the camper slowed as Cavallero made a sharp turn to the right. We were entering the vineyard of Angelo Musso, sacred soil to my father and his friends. For fifty years they had quaffed the genial Chianti and claret from the vines of those rocky hills. Not only were they Angelo's customers, they were in fact his slaves, anguished when his crop failed, for his wine was the milk of their second childhood, delivered to the customer's back door in gallon jugs once a month, the empties carried back to the winery.

Every five years or so a freeze destroyed the vines or the new wine turned inexplicably sour and the pàisani had to switch to another brand. It brought despair among them, and insomnia and rheumatism. To a man, Angelo's customers lived in dread that he might die before them.

The tires crackled in the gravel driveway as we pulled to the side of the Musso house and piled out of the car. A very nice house it was, a stone house of two stories built by my father a long time ago. Massive grapevines covered it now, climbing up the chimney atop the slanted tile roof. A roar, like the distant sound of traffic, made the air throb. It was the bees, thousands of them, humming moodily in the vines, a funereal mmmmmm sound when you tuned your attention to the mournful cadence of their mysterious dirge that seemed to lift the house off the ground and hold it in melancholy suspension.

Next to the house stood a thick grape arbor, so impenetrable it blocked out the hot sunshine, and beneath it, at the end of a long picnic table, sat Angelo Musso, eighty-four years old, a shriveled, bald gnome of a man, sun-blackened, with tawny muscat eyes. His chair was a beat-up, overstuffed mohair, so low the old man's chin was barely above the table level.

Angelo Musso could not utter a word, for his cancerous voice box had been excised ten years earlier. Cigarette ash left a trail of gray down the front of his blue shirt, and he coughed intermittently, for he was a chain smoker, with two packs of Camels on the table in front of him, as well as a carafe of wine, a cigarette lighter and an overflowing ashtray.

For my father and most of the old-time Italians in Placer County Angelo Musso was extra special, an ancient oracle who dispensed no wisdom, a sage who gave no advice, a prophet without predictions, and a god who fermented the most enchanting wine in the world on a tiny thirty-acre vineyard endowed with large boulders and sublime vines. That made him divine. So did his enforced silence. Because he could not speak, everyone came to him with their problems. And everyone found solutions in his yellowish eyes.

We approached him reverently, monks in single file paying homage to their abbot, bowing, lifting his mummified, blue-veined hand and kissing it solemnly. The others spoke to him in whispered Italian, congratulating him on his good health, saying he seemed to grow younger with each passing year, causing him to smile with toothless delight.

My father introduced me, and though the old man had seen me many times, he failed to recognize me then. Bowing to the custom, I kissed what seemed only bones and parchment in his hand, noticed the yellowish fingers, and smelled the nicotine-drenched skin.

As we took seats at the long table Angelo tapped the wine carafe with a spoon. At the bell-like tinkle, the kitchen door opened and a woman appeared, carrying a tray of food and wine. She was short, ponderous, and graceful as an elephant, whirling down upon us quickly, dispensing glass tumblers, two pitchers of wine, and plates of bread and provolone cheese. She looked about fifty, her massive body giving her head the appearance of smallness, and she had hardly any neck at all. Her costume was bib overalls over a T-shirt and a frilly cocktail apron around her waist. She had a mustache too, a dim fuzz that matched her black hair. I stared in fascination. I had never seen her before.

"Odette, the housekeeper," my father whispered.

Swiftly Odette served the guests, pirouetting around the table and back into the kitchen.

Out of respect for Angelo's muteness we did not speak as we ate and drank, and this I thought strange; after all, there was nothing wrong with Angelo's hearing. But we tossed kisses his way to show our pleasure with the chilled wine, the homemade mozzarella and the Italian bread. Now the bees came, one or two at a time in advance parties, then swarms to investigate Angelo's guests, settling on our shirts, our arms, the rims of the glasses and carafes. They formed a little halo around Angelo's gray hair and helped themselves to his cheese and wine, and he seemed to enjoy their company.

Soon I too drew their attention, two or three at first, circling, tasting, sniffing, then a howling mob. They were in my hair and on my ears, on my hands and along my neck, and I remembered the crabs and I trembled with a creeping fear and a desire to bolt for open country, holding my breath, resisting panic, knowing they would clobber me if I made a run for it.

Angelo cackled at my plight, a chicken noise in his dead throat, his waning eyes flickering like candles.

"Take it easy," my father warned. "Be friends with them. Get acquainted."

They did not sting me, they were simply putting me on, and most of them flew away as suddenly as they had arrived. We got down to deep meditative drinking, the witchery of the wine transcending the miracle of its taste, enveloping our souls within the cocoon of the humming bees, a sweet droning, the vintage plentiful and cool in those warm hills as Hypnos descended and time passed to the drone of the bees.

I slept about an hour, my head in my arms, my arms on the table. Wakening, bombs detonated in my skull and my eyes tried to burst their sockets. My father sat mumbling to himself, dipping a finger into his wine glass and sucking it foolishly. I saw Cavallaro stumbling in the hot sunshine, walking drunkenly toward us in the grape arbor, trying to zip his fly and not succeeding. Zarlingo was gone and so was our ancient host.

I craved water, cold water on my face, on my body, a creek, a pond, a horse trough, cool cleanliness, and I got up and staggered out into the sun toward the winery a hundred yards away, a stone building like the house. What had happened? Why had I drunk so much? To sip a glass of wine, and a second glass, and even a third, yes. But to drown in it, to drink beyond satiety, to gorge in the heat of the day, to tempt death quietly, silently, in the company of drunken old men — mama mia!

The heavy, planked winery door squealed on its hinges as Zarlingo emerged, blinded by the sun, and lurched into me. He was pale, his face textured in misery. Like a zombie he shoved me aside and wandered back toward the house, one hand clutching his belt. I watched him weave away. His pants were on backward.

As I turned, Odette faced me in the winery door and I backed away in surprise. She smiled with her charming mustache.

"Hello, buster . . ."

I said, "Hi."

"You want some action?"

She reached for my fly and I backed away.

"God, no."

"Any way you want it. I suck too."

"Pass."

I stepped away and hurried down the path, past the winery and out into the vineyard. On a hill two hundred yards away I saw oscillating sprinklers forming a rainbow as they pulsed jets of water upon a field of grape stumps sprouting new buds. I scrambled up to the section, peeled off my clothes, and stood naked at the end of the rainbow. It was a summer shower, refreshing my soul, nostalgic, a day in Italy, the hills of Tuscany, and I was sober again as I put on my clothes.

Back at Angelo's house I found Zarlingo and Cavallaro asleep in the cab of the truck. My father wasn't around. I went to the kitchen door and knocked several times. Finally I stepped inside a large, disorderly kitchen. Odette was not a good housekeeper. The sink was full of dirty dishes, and an open garbage pail occupied the center of the room. Asleep on a studio couch, his dentures and his cigarettes on a table beside him, was Angelo.

I went outside again. Coming along the path from the winery were Odette and my old man. He had the legs of a rag doll. Her arm was around his waist and she laughed as she carried him along. He was sound asleep, his shirttail hanging out. Odette and I boosted him into the driver's seat, and as his butt loomed before me I slammed him with my knee as hard as I could, and I was glad, glad, glad.

15

By NECESSITY it became my turn to drive, with Zarlingo back in the wheelbarrow and my father up front between me and Cavallaro. We left the hill country, the orchards and the vineyards, and began to climb toward the Sierra peaks. The old man slept deeply on my shoulder, his breath as sour as one of Angelo Musso's barrels.

After a while the air grew colder, and lowering, white mists tumbled down to the highway. I opened the window and tattered pieces of clouds whisked through my father's hair. The air was good for him, cold in his nostrils and lungs, and he wakened and looked around, his eyes like crushed cherries. He wanted a cigar.

The road dipped and it was on the downgrade a couple of miles to a place called Alp Hollow. There was a grocery store and one small cabin. I stopped in front of the store and my father and Cavallaro tumbled out like sacks of kindling — you heard the crackle of their bones. Growling like a beast, Zarlingo crawled from the camper. The three bumbled their way into a cathedral of superb pines, in different directions, and urinated, each against a tree, secretly, furtively, swaying like sleepwalkers, their backs to one another, too modest to flash their cocks.

Zarlingo and Cavallaro returned to the truck, but my father marched stiffly into the grocery store. He returned puffing on a cigar, a package under his arm. With grotesque drunken dignity he came to the camper and nearly fell on his face as he climbed into the seat.

"Let's move!" he ordered, like some fool in command of other fools. I gave him my ugliest glance, sickened by his glut for booze, his abuse of his last handful of days.

With a demonic smile he opened the paper sack. It was a pint of brandy. He looked at me and laughed at my loathing of him, and I felt anger and disgust. As he put the bottle to his mouth I snatched it from his hand and flung it out the window. It exploded against a stone. He was surprised, but he didn't breathe a word. Flicking the ash from his cigar, his crazed red eyes drilled at the windshield as he slashed off a slew of soft Italian curses, something about America and dogshit.

It was six o'clock now, the sun long gone from Alp Hollow, and it was cold with the quickening night, but as we climbed out of there sunlight made a wedding cake of the snow peaks as Highway 80 snaked eastward and up to 7,000 feet. The dying sun at our backs, we cruised through lonesome mountain hamlets — Emigrant Gap, Cisco, Soda Springs, Donner Pass.

Beyond the pass my father cautioned me to slow down. "It's up ahead a little ways."

I scanned the terrain for signs of the Monte Casino golf course — the greens with waving flags, the golfers, the rolling fairways, the clubhouse. Truth was, in the back of my mind the most compelling reason for making the trip was the golf course. Looking around, all I saw on both sides of the highway was a vast ocean of pines, tall and impenetrable, flowing into infinity.

"I don't see the golf course, Papa."

He looked ahead without speaking.

"Where's the golf course?"

"They ain't any."

"You said there was a golf course."

"No golf course."

"How come?"

"So I said so. So sue me."

"Why did you say it?"

"'Less I said it, you wouldn't come."

He turned to me in pain and embarrassment, battered eyes, battered man, and I had a sudden flashback, and he was nine years old in an impoverished Italian village, trapped by his father in some boyish fabrication, with the same injured expression his face now showed. A sad business, the way the creases shaped themselves on the face into unerasable furrows. I hated the sorrow upon his face. I liked him better when he was arrogant, selfish, tough, a bastard to the core. I slapped his knee.

"It's okay," I smiled. "I would have come anyway."

His hand trembled as he struck a match and put it to his cigar that was already lit.

"No tennis, either?" I smiled.

"No tennis."

"No swimming pool?"

"Nope."

"How about the bears, and the timber wolves?"

He tried to laugh and almost succeeded.

The Monte Casino Lodge was not a lodge at all. It was a motel. A quarter of a mile down a side road off the highway we came to a clearing in the deep woods. A dozen log cabins were scattered among the trees, most of them with cars parked alongside. But for the cars, the scene could have been a settlers' village a hundred years before, smoke trailing from cabin chimneys and hanging heavily among the trees, the odor of bacon and beefsteak permeating the chilling air. A red neon sign spelling OFFICE over the porch of the far cabin spoiled the primitive scene.

We pulled up before the porch and my father hit the horn a couple of times. It brought Sam Ramponi from inside. He was a squat, balloon-bellied man of seventy with the body of a bear and the face of a wolf. With a yell of joyous recognition he rushed toward us as my father and Cavallaro got out of the car. No doubt about it, Sam Ramponi belonged to the brotherhood of the grape, his heavy face streaked with purple cobwebs of broken blood vessels, his grinning mouth sporting big, repulsive dentures. There was much laughter and handshaking, and when Zarlingo dropped from the camper the jollity began again, backslapping, guffaws, embraces — a class reunion — for Sam Ramponi was a San Elmo man, a retired brakeman who longed for the good old days when the Café Roma was the center of the universe and the world had not turned into *merde*.

He stared warmly as my father introduced us.

"My oldest boy. He's my helper."

Ramponi grabbed my hand.

"Hello, Tony. I remember you now! The best football player San Elmo ever had."

My name wasn't Tony and I had never played high school football, but the man was only trying to be friendly.

"You, boy!" my father barked. "Get this here truck unloaded." It was his ugliest flaw: the boss, the big-shot syndrome. "Drive around back of those cabins. You'll see some stone and a pile of sand. Unload there. And be careful with my tools. Cover them up, in case it rains."

His three friends were impressed, staring in silence. "Right on, sir!" I saluted, and climbed into the truck.

Ramponi herded his friends toward the office.

"Come on, you suckers. Let's play cards."

16

IT WAS DARK when I finished unloading the truck. A pumpkin moon slipped above the treetops, lighting up the site of the new smokehouse — a freshly poured concrete slab. My father was right. It was going to be a small uncomplicated job and we would be out of there in about ten days.

A NO VACANCY sign blazed above the porch as I brought the truck back to the motel office and parked. I went inside, past the desk and into the kitchen, where a poker game was in progress, the four paisani seated around a table covered with a white oilcloth. Mrs. Ramponi, a brittle, diminutive woman, was serving wine from an Angelo Musso jug. She was quite frail, clasping the jug to her bosom with both arms as she poured, her skin the color of wax beans, her scalp beneath thinning white hair shining under the overhead drop light.

The way Sam Ramponi treated his wife, Gloria Steinem would have gunned him down on the spot. He did not trouble to introduce me, and when she nodded, smiling with broken teeth, I said hello.

"Give him a drink," Sam said.

Mrs. Ramponi placed the jug on the sideboard in order to free her hands and offer me a glass. I thanked her as she poured.

"You're welcome," she said.

"Out," Sam ordered.

At once she crossed the kitchen to an open bedroom and sat in the semidarkness near the door, arms folded, awaiting further orders. She reminded me of the old women attendants in the men's washrooms of Rome nightclubs. I thought of joining the card game for a while, but obviously I was an outsider, not of their generation, and nobody invited me to sit down. But I moved closer to the table and watched the play. Ramponi put a fresh cigar into his mouth and searched for a match. She was there at his side immediately, holding a match under his stiffened jaw.

"Cabin seven," he said. "Turn mattress. Change sheets for Nick and son."

She left at once.

Sam Ramponi dealt the cards. It was draw poker, open on anything, two-bit limit. The chips were for nickels, dimes and quarters. So far it was an even game, everyone with about the same number of chips.

When Zarlingo picked up his cards I saw that he held a pair of queens and an ace, not bad for openers in a small, sociable game. But he said, "Pass."

The others passed too. The pot was sweetened with another dime from each player, Ramponi dealing. Again I looked down at Zarlingo's hand. This time he held a pair of kings and an ace.

"Pass," he said.

They all passed and four more dimes were added to the pot. It was that kind of a game, tight-assed, cutthroat poker, building up the stakes, waiting for the nuts. Fortunately for my old man, the stakes were small and limited. He was too volatile for poker, too impatient, a born loser playing in the wrong game. And yet, alas, it was his favorite game. He liked to charge in there boldly. The patience of his opponents, their stoicism, steamed him into rash decisions. A bad hand, and he sagged in despair. Three aces and he was grinning from ear to ear. Trapped and beaten, he was too proud to drop out and tried to bluff. And then they shafted him. I had witnessed it so many times I marveled they could take his money.

Tonight it did not seem that kind of a game, nor would it last long. He, Zarlingo and Cavallaro were haggard from exhaustion, bodies crumpled from dissipation. They had drunk wine the night before and most of that day, and now they were juiced again on Angelo's grapes.

Mrs. Ramponi returned and handed me the key to Cabin 7. "I hope you'll be comfortable," she said, standing there a moment, pretending to watch the game. Ramponi frowned at her.

"Food," he said.

Immediately Mrs. Ramponi produced a loaf of bread and a jar of mayonnaise. That Ramponi! Eyes in the back of his head, for she was behind him as she began to spread mayonnaise for sandwiches.

"Butter," he said.

She brought out the butter. I gave Zarlingo the keys to his truck and backed toward the door. The poker hand was a showdown between my father and Ramponi. My father spread out kings and queens: two pair. Ramponi spread three deuces and swept up the pot.

I said good night to everyone, but the gamblers ignored me as I started for the door. Without enthusiasm, without sincerity, Ramponi called, "Hey, Tony. Sure you won't play a hand or two?"

"Let him go to bed," my father said. "He's got a big day tomorrow."

17

THE NIGHT WAS cold and misty. From half a dozen cabins came the voice of Archie Bunker insulting his wife, the audience shrieking with delight. No doubt about it, Archie belonged in that poker game, his kind of people.

I carried the luggage and a sack of tools from the truck to Cabin 7. The accommodations were routine motel décor: a kitchen with a bar, a divan, a rug, a couple of chairs, a TV and a bed.

The bed I did not like. It was a double bed and it meant I would have to sleep with the old man. Fretting, I sat on it and considered the dilemma. I had never slept with my father. I had rarely in my life even touched him, except for a rare handshake over the years, and now I had no desire to sleep with him. I considered his old bones, his old skin, the lonely, ornery oldness of him, the wine-soaked oldness of him and his sodden, sinful friends, the son of a bitch he had been: unreasonable, tyrannical, boorish, profligate wop who had trapped me on this snafu safari into the mountains, far from wife and home and work, all for his bedizened vanity, to prove to himself he was still a hotshot stonemason.

Then it all began to come back. I was ten years old at a street dance in San Elmo, the night of the Fourth of July. I was in the alley behind the dance, searching trash barrels. In the darkness I saw a man and woman making love against a telephone post, the woman holding up her dress, the man throwing his body at her. I knew what they were doing, but it scared me as I crouched behind a pile of crates. Hand in hand the man and woman walked toward me. The man was my father. The woman was Della Lorenzo, who lived two doors from our house with her husband and two sons, my classmates in school. After that I never played with the Lorenzo kids again. I was ashamed to look into their eyes. I hated my father. I hated Mrs. Lorenzo; she was so common, so frumpy and plain. I hated the Lorenzo house, their yard. I kicked their mongrel dog. I strangled one of their chickens. When Mrs. Lorenzo died of breast cancer the next year I was indifferent. She had it coming. No doubt she was in hell, making a place for my father.

Easter Sunday. I was twelve. We were at the Santucci farm, the entire family. Hordes of Italians from all over the county, long tables sagging with wine, pasta, salad and roast goat, my old man with a goat's head on his plate, eating the brains and the eyes, laughing and showing off before women screaming in horror. Afterward, a softball game. Somebody hit a ball over the hedge in the outfield. I leaped after it and landed on top of my father, hidden in the tall grass, his bare bottom white as a winter moon as he pumped Mrs. Santucci, who was supposed to be my mother's best friend. Astounded, I ran toward the orchard, over the creek, down the pear grove. My father came racing after me. I had the speed of a deer. I knew he would never catch me, but he did. He shook me. He was throwing spit in his rage. "One word to your mother and by God I'll kill you!"

I spent the rest of the long afternoon at my mother's side while she gossiped on the lawn with the other ladies. I would not leave her. I sat on the grass and clutched the hem of her dress and it annoyed her. "Go play with the other kids," she said. "You're bothering me."

No. I would not lie down in the mountain darkness beside that abominable old man, rewarding him with affection and companionship after a lifetime of unrepentant sensuality at the expense of his wife and family. No wonder my poor mother thought of divorce, and Virgil was ashamed of him, and Mario fled from the sight of him, and Stella disapproved of him.

I found an extra blanket in the closet, kicked off my shoes, and curled up on the divan. Hours later I wakened to voices outside, drunken laughter, the banging of car doors. I went to the window and watched Zarlingo and Cavallaro drive off in the Datsun. It crept along, barely moving in the deep mist as my father ran alongside, waving his arms and shouting, "Turn on your lights!"

The lights speared the mist and the car crawled away. The disappearing taillights through the forest road promised certain doom. I was sure the old dudes would never make it back to San Elmo, that they would drift off the road into some canyon wasteland. But I was wrong. They made it home in four days, traveling ninety-five miles by easy stages, stopping at every saloon that popped up along the perilous route.

It was after one o'clock when my father tumbled into the cabin. He switched on the ugly light in the globed overhead chandelier, left the door open, and marched straight to the bed, where he collapsed. In thirty seconds he was deeply asleep, his breathing heavy, his mouth open. I locked the door, peeled off his clothes, and rolled him under the covers. As I turned off the light and lay down on the divan he began to moan, "Mama mia, mama mia."

Then he was sobbing. Was this any way for a man to fall asleep, calling for his mother? It seemed he would never stop. It tore me to shreds. I knew nothing of his mother. She had been dead for over sixty years, had expired in Italy after he had left and come to America, still visiting him now in his old man's sleep, as if he felt her near in his dreams, like one lost and wandering, crying for her.

I lay there tearing my hair and thinking. Stop it, Father, you are drunk and full of self-pity and you must stop it, you have no right to cry, you are my father and the right to cry belongs to my wife and children, to my mother, for it is obscene that you should cry, it humiliates me, I shall die from your grief, I cannot endure your pain, I should be spared your pain for I have enough of my own. I shall have more too, but I shall never cry before others, I shall be strong and face my last days without tears, old man. I need your life and not your death, your joy and not your dismay.

Then I was crying too, on my feet, crossing to him. I gathered his limp head in my arms (as I had seen my mother do), I wiped his tears with a corner of the sheet, I rocked him like a child, and soon he was no longer crying, and I eased him gently to the pillow and he slept quietly.

18

He was somber and wretched in the morning, eyes smoldering beneath the ashes of the night before. Dangerous he was, breathing pain, hostile to the dreary prospects of a gray, new day. He began with the usual ritual of the wine, removing one of the gallon jugs from a cardboard carton and tilting it on his elbow, sucking with the greed of an infant. He turn to growl at me as he corked the jug.

"Get up. Time to work."

I sat up and reached for my jeans. He crossed to the window and stared at a bleak, foggy world.

"I don't like this place," he complained. "I musta been crazy to take this job."

"Let's shove it, then. Let's just leave."

"Only thing to do is get out as fast as we can. Four or five days."

"I thought you said ten days."

"Get some breakfast. We got work to do."

As he left there was activity in the parkway, car motors coughing and wheezing in the thin, cold atmosphere as the motel guests began to drive off. It felt like impending snow as I stepped outside, clouds bloated and hanging low, a dismal and remote corner of the earth. Down south at this hour I would be in bed still, bright sunshine through my window and a view of the sea. I would put on a robe and have my first of ten cups of coffee, contemplating a walk along the warm deserted beach or perhaps a sunbath, altogether a dreamy day of rest and calculated indolence, putting off an hour or two of work to the late afternoon when it could no longer be avoided.

Though the motel had no restaurant, our arrangement with Ramponi included board and room. I crossed through the office to the kitchen, where Mrs. Ramponi was preparing my breakfast, my father having told her I was on my way. We said good morning and I sat at the table and asked if my father had eaten a good breakfast.

"Brandy and coffee. It's all he wanted."

She looked fresher than the night before, with the clean, well-soaped complexion of a Swede or German, pale eyes and white eyebrows. When Ramponi wasn't around to crush her she was vivacious and pleasant and not bad-looking for an older woman. She wore a blue scarf around her soft hair, her figure covered by the kind of apron worn by hotel porters, full length with many pockets. A place was set at the table, and she served me a breakfast steak with two eggs and toast and coffee.

Mrs. Ramponi was loquacious, eager to talk, a workhorse who loved to chatter about her tasks, for she did everything around there: registering guests, carrying luggage, cleaning the rooms, doing the laundry, keeping the books, managing the whole setup. She said Sam never lifted a finger to help her.

"Why not?"

"He works in Reno."

"Reno?"

"He deals blackjack at the Blue Nugget."

I savored the excellent steak and thought of last night's poker game at that very table — Sam Ramponi, a cold sober, professional card dealer matching his skill against three old friends drunk out of their skulls. Sam must have wiped them out of what their wallets held, which wasn't very much.

Mrs. Ramponi watched me put away the last of the steak. "There's more," she coaxed, lifting a sizzling piece from the griddle and ladling it to my plate.

"You're a hell of a cook, Mrs. Ramponi."

She tossed her head in a pixie way.

"I'm a hell of anything I choose to be," she laughed. "You may think I'm just a maid around here, Sam Ramponi's old woman, but believe me, I'm not!"

Her eyes zoomed in on me steadily, searchingly, and I felt the gentle strum of my libido. It startled me. Was this sweet, blue-eyed old lady making a pass? Impossible. Women never made passes at me anymore, not even my wife. Of late, the only action coming my way was from some reveries on paper, hot off my typewriter.

I evaded her scrutiny and kept busy cutting my steak.

"Tell me, Mrs. Ramponi, why the smokehouse?"

"Why, to smoke meat, of course. Venison."

"Sam hunts deer?"

"I do the hunting in this family," she said proudly.

She was so small, so prim and genteel, I found it hard to believe. "You don't look the type."

"What type?"

"The hunter type, stalking deer."

"I don't stalk them. I shoot them from my back porch. Just sprinkle a little grain over the snow and they follow it to the door. Then I let 'em have it." She gave her elbow a jerk, as if firing a rifle.

"That's entrapment. It's against the law."

"Not if they trample your crops."

I had to smile. "What crops, Mrs. Ramponi?"

She folded her arms.

"I grow lots of things up here. Besides, I don't hear you complaining about the steaks you wolfed down. That was entrapment too. Got him from ten feet. Right between the eyes."

I controlled myself. I couldn't say anything. My plate was empty. The meat was inside of me. Where had that angelic old lady come by her killer instinct? Maybe she was killing Sam Ramponi vicariously.

"I don't believe you," I said, rising. "You're simply not the kind of a person who'd shoot down a hungry deer. It's not your nature. I *know!* You're much too fine a human being."

She frowned, mulling it over as I turned and walked out. She hurried after me. "Be quick about that smokehouse!" she demanded. "I'll be needing it any day now, quick as it snows."

I found old Nick seated on a rock, sharpening wooden stakes with a hatchet. "Hey," I said. "How'd you do in that poker game?"

"Who wants to know?"

"I have a particular reason for wanting to know."

"You win some, you lose some." He nodded toward the pile of sand. "Screen some sand."

"You know Sam Ramponi is a pro, that he runs a game in Reno?"

"So what else is new?"

"He took you guys, didn't he?"

"He got eight dollars offa me."

"How about Lou and Zarlingo?"

He pointed. "See that shovel? Use it."

The sun jumped out from behind the mist; the clouds scattered, driven off, and the warmth poured down. We were in an enchanting spot, an island in the forest, the land cleared to the border of giant trees. No wonder there were deer. A little stream bisected the property, giggling over stones in the shallow water. The Ramponi cabin was only fifty yards away, the kitchen window overlooking a view of the clearing. And there I was, screening sand to make the mortar to hold the stones in the walls that formed the slaughterhouse to smoke the deer that Mrs. Ramponi shot by luring them to her window. I screened sand and thought, oh, shit, what am I doing here?

The old man began to move around, going from corner to corner of the slab, driving stakes and securing a plumb line to them. It was a simple operation, but it left him puffing, and he returned to the stone and sat down. He took off his battered brown hat and sweat seeped out of his hair.

"Go get the jug," he said.

I looked at my left palm and saw my first blister.

"It's too early in the day," I said.

It stung him and he put his thumb in his mouth and snapped it toward me, a scurrilous Italian gesture the meaning of which I never found out, though he had done it three or four times a day throughout his life. My guess was that it meant: up your ass. Then he clumped off sullenly toward the cabins.

I stood sucking my blister and examining the pile of stones. They were chunks of rough-hewn granite, gray and misshapen. I bent down to heft one of the smaller stones. Not that it was heavy, it was preposterously, unbelievably heavy, at least a hundred pounds, and no bigger than a basketball. The others were like it or heavier. I could help him lift the smaller stones to the wall, but it was going to be a killer job for a man of seventy-six with soft hands and soft muscles who had done no physical labor in five years. He could sprain his back, or pop a hernia, or break a blood vessel. I had observed the flaming veins of his eyes. The wine had been thorough and the damage had been done. It was madness to challenge the danger, but my old man was mad, the burden of his uselessness was madness, and the sense of his entire life coming to an end in a struggle with stones was the maddest part of it all.

Why was he doing this job? A smokehouse for the curing of deer meat! Chances were that twenty years ago he would have turned the job down as too remote from his home, too insignificant for his pride.

He could of course go another route in his final days, getting smashed daily at the Café Roma. Or slouched in the parlor watching television, enduring the cackle of his wife hovering over him with plates of pasta as she speculated on the joys and sorrows of widowhood. Or he could sit on the front porch overlooking Pleasant Street, watching the exciting spectacle of an occasional dog or human being passing by. Or cultivate tomatoes and green peppers in the backyard. Not Nick Molise. He wanted a wall to build — that was it. He didn't care what wall it was, but let it be a wall that brought respect from his friends who knew he was abroad in the world, a workingman, a builder.

He returned from the cabin swinging the jug and looking better, looking pleased. He offered me a drink and I took a mouthful.

"Keep it cool in the creek," he said, and I lowered the jug into the chill water and let it sink to the shallow bottom.

We mixed the mortar and I carried a bucketful to the mortarboard at the corner of the slab. He stirred it with his trowel, sloshed and slurped it around to get it to the right consistency. Then he pointed to one of the smaller stones.

"That one."

I hefted it to the slab. He troweled a bed of mortar and took the stone from my grasp, his hands about it. That was the moment of truth. His face purpled and his eyes wanted to explode as he let go the stone and dropped to his knees. He tried again. This time he was able to imbed the stone into the mortar, but he was cursing in Italian, cursing the stone, the world, himself. I watched and he did not like it, and he cursed me too.

Trying to soothe him, I said, "Don't worry, you're a little out of shape, that's all."

"Shut up." He pointed wth the trowel. "That one."

It was another hundred-pounder. I gathered it up.

"Tell you what, Papa. You spread the mortar and I'll lay the stone."

"Shut up."

He unfurled the mortar and took the stone from my arms, fighting it bitterly, overwhelmed by it, even though he got it properly positioned.

After two hours we had used up the small stones and he tried to stand erect, but his lower back was unhinged and he could not make it. Bent like an ape, he shambled to the creek bank and lifted out the jug. He eased himself to his belly on the ground and pulled at the cold wine. His face sagged mournfully, his eyes sunk in disappointment. The forest looked down and comprehended his plight. The trees sighed. Birds gossiped in alarm. The sky stared in compassionate blue. My father, my poor old man! He was beaten and he knew it, but he would not admit it. He had built his share of things with stone, churches and schools and at least one library, but now he was having a hell of a time putting up a ten-foot smokehouse with no windows and only one door.

Let defeat sink in, I thought, let him face the fact that it is beyond his strength and his years, let him throw in the trowel so that he can get the hell off this mountain and go home. God bless the deer!

Flopping down beside him, I took the jug. That wine! It renewed my mouth, my flesh, my skin, my heart and soul, and I thanked God for Angelo Musso's hills. We sprawled in silence, listening to the birds, passing the jug.

I asked what he had in mind.

"We have to bust the rocks, make little ones out of big ones."

Mrs. Ramponi appeared, carrying sandwiches and a bowl of fresh strawberries on a tray.

"Lunchtime," she said.

My father ripped a bite from his sandwich without so much as a glance at it. "Good," he said, putting it aside and going for the jug again.

I opened my sandwich suspiciously. It was ham and mayonnaise. Mrs. Ramponi watched in annoyance. "What'd you think it was, deer meat?"

No matter what it was, I could not eat it.

She turned to my father. "Nick, you look tired. Why don't you go back to the cabin and sleep a while? No use killing yourself on the first day."

"That's right," he said.

She turned and walked back to the motel. I pulled off my shoes and dipped my feet into the creek. There was only one way to sabotage the Ramponi smokehouse and that was not to build it. I looked at my father. He was asleep, with a sandwich dangling from his fingers. I shook him.

"Go take a nap for a while."

He rose painfully and walked on unsure legs toward the motel. I sat with my feet in the creek, eating the strawberries. Then I dozed off, and when I wakened the old man had not returned. I put on my shoes and socks and started for our cabin. He wasn't there. But I spotted him through the kitchen window. He was coming stealthily from the back door of Cabin 6. Mrs. Ramponi followed. He moved toward the smokehouse and she went off toward the motel office. I waited for the old man to move out of sight in the trees and then I ran to the office. I didn't know what had happened between them in Cabin 6, probably nothing, but she was not good for my father and I hated her anyway. I rang the bell in the office and she appeared from the kitchen.

"Leave my father alone," I said.

"What on earth are you talking about?"

I was unreasonable but I didn't care. "Just keep your hands off my father."

Her mouth curled in scorn.

"If you were half the man your father is, you wouldn't dare talk to me like that. Get out, you creep."

I backed out, ashamed, sick at myself, wondering what the hell was happening to me. I blamed the altitude, 7,000 feet of it. Bizarre creatures were seen in these uncanny forests, gnomes, the ghosts of old prospectors, lost survivors of the Donner party, even the tracks of Big Foot. It was getting to me.

Back at the smokehouse my father seemed invigorated, and the kink in his back was gone as he selected a long-handled sledgehammer and positioned himself before a craggy chunk of granite four feet square. He was about to make little ones out of big ones. I stood aside and watched him swing the sledge powerfully, half a dozen blows until the stone began to break, not in clean sheaths, but twisted, jagged chunks and splinters.

''Fine,'' he pronounced, breathing hard, ''just fine. Bring them to the wall.''

I hauled them and he laid them, the big ones and the little ones, the chunks and the splinters. I crushed the rock and he did the wall. We did fine. When tired, he called for wine. He could not straighten up, so he stood like an ape as he drank. When he began to sweat the blotches on his back and under his arms were rose-colored. I thought, what the hell, it's nutritious, it's grape sugar, energy, and drank with him every time. We were doing fine, fine. We were tired and dazed, and I thought I saw a gnome with a red hat in the forest as the sun went over the trees and the smokehouse wall sprouted toward the sky.

We stopped work as darkness fell. We could have worked by moonlight, but that would have been the edge of madness. Sam Ramponi might drive home from Reno and laugh at us. Motel guests would wonder what was going on. We called it a day. We had drunk two gallons. We had pissed three or four. We were spinning. We were spooked. Old Nick laughed to himself. He fell on his face as we went for our supper. I laughed and pulled him to his feet. Ramponi wasn't home. Mrs. Ramponi filled our plates. Maybe it was deer meat. What did I care?

My father fell asleep at the table. I dragged him to the cabin and heaped him into bed. I slept. Suddenly it was morning. No need to dress; I had slept in my clothes. My mouth was full of Mrs. Ramponi's old tennis shoes and dog hair. I cleansed it with a gargle of wine and we went back to work.

We hurried now. We had to get out of there. I busted the big stones and the old man popped them into the wall. We were at sea, on a raft, hurrying, setting a record. Have a drink, son. It was a race. Have a drink, Papa. No starting line, no finish. But fast. He tossed aside the plumb line. He stopped using the mason's level. He worked by instinct. Sometimes he lowered his head down to the line of the wall and squinted, keeping it plumb. The wall went up and the wine went down. Once I looked up at the sky and asked, "What time is it?" He answered, "There ain't no time," and I laughed. God, he was profound. When the wine was gone Ramponi brought more from Reno. Just in time. In the last moment of the last drop from the last jug. Good wine, from Angelo Musso.

19

THEN A peculiar thing happened. My father died. We were working away, swirling in mortar and stone, and all of a sudden I
sensed that he had left the world. I sought his face and it was
written there. His eyes were open, his hands moved, he splashed
mortar, but he was dead, and in death he had nothing to say.
Sometimes he drifted off like a specter into the trees to take a piss.
How could he be dead, I wondered, and still walk off and pee? A
ghost he was, a goner, a stiff. I wanted to ask him if he was well, if
by chance he was still alive, but I was too tired and too busy dying
myself, and too tired of making phrases. I could see the question
on paper, typewritten, with quotation marks, but it was too
heavy to verbalize. Besides, what difference did it make? We all
had to die someday.

On the fourth day, between large draughts of Angelo Musso,
we built the scaffold and had two feet to go. Nick, who was dead,
could feel no pain as he strung out the stone. He was not neat
anymore, not the fussy, fastidious stonemason of the past, and
the wall was splattered and the mortar oozed and made big pies at
the base. There below, still alive, I broke slabs and packed them

on my shoulder and lifted them to the scaffold, and then one day, I know not which day, I died too.

I must have died bravely and quietly, for I did not remember lamentation and tears. First there was this splintering pain in my lumbar region from swinging the sledge and then it was gone, it seemed to drift off into the forest, as did the other pains — my aching feet, my blistered palms, the throb in my kidneys — one by one they all vanished, and I felt the cessation of the nervous system. When I die again, I thought, and undoubtedly for the last time, I must remember to face it as I did that day in the mountains, succumbing to death as if she were my beloved, smiling as I took her into my arms.

The other deceased person, my friend, my old man, greeted me across the threshold of life with eyes vacant as windowpanes as I hoisted him a massive stone and he wrestled it into a nest of mortar.

Then an ironic thing occurred. Turning from the scaffold, I stepped upon the sharp edge of a hoe and it sprang at me with its handle, a brutal clout between the eyes. I felt no pain at all. The blow knocked me down, but I was beyond pain.

We did not see much of Sam Ramponi except in the morning as he drove off to Reno, sometimes waving, sometimes not. Toward evening on the fifth day he strolled up without a sound and stood close to the construction, his arms folded, staring at my father on the scaffold. No greeting, no sign of recognition from either man. My father returned Ramponi's concerned frown with mournful but defiant eyes. Ramponi could not have known of our demise, but he sensed a change in us, an immateriality, spectral and disembodied. He waved me an uneasy glance and hurried away toward the motel, turning once to look over his shoulder at us, like someone repelled.

Mrs. Ramponi was puzzled and disturbed too. Whereas at first she brought our lunches to the job, she now placed the tray on a tree stump fifty feet from where we worked, and then scurried back to the motel. At breakfast she shrank from serving us, showing a fearsome respect. We usually left by the kitchen door, which she promptly bolted shut as we walked out.

Sunday afternoon, six days from the start, my father laid the final stone and the smokehouse was finished. We were bearded and gray, we were drunk and we stank, for we had worked and slept in the same clothes.

Kneeling beside the creek, we pulled on the jug and gazed with sunken eyes at what we had wrought — a chunky little structure that resembled an Arab bunker in the Sinai. It was crude and it was crooked. The stones appeared to have been thrown into the wall rather than set. The walls waved crazily, convex and concave, bellied in and bellied out, and they were very thick, much thicker than Papa had agreed upon. Mortar oozed from the joints, soiling the walls. Whatever its aesthetic flaws, the building looked indestructible. All that remained for completion were the roof and the placement of the single door, tasks for a carpenter. Molise and son were finished.

The area was in ruins, like a deserted battlefield. It badly needed cleaning up, if only to lend a little dignity to the loony smokehouse. Planks were scattered about, odds and ends of lumber and chunks of stone, tools, empty wine jugs, cement sacks, paper plates and napkins, half-eaten sandwiches, clothing. The more my eyes fell upon the smokehouse the crazier it seemed.

It didn't look like a building at all, but more like a load of stone carelessly dumped there. Tired, drunk and hallucinating, I began to see it as an ancient Indian burial. Then an iceberg. I blinked and looked again. It was a polar bear. Now it was Mount Whitney, now a rocky formation on the moon. A mist settled over the clearing as I rolled up the hoses and gathered the tools. When I looked at the thing again it was a ship moving slowly across a fogbound sea. Disquieting and vague alarms sent me hurrying toward the cabins.

Through the mist Sam Ramponi's Cadillac entered the motel driveway. He pulled up beside me. He was in his working clothes, Reno black silk suit, white shirt, black bow tie.

"How you doin'?" he asked.

"All finished."

He sighed. "Good. How does she look?"

"It's a smokehouse, Sam. There's no denying that."

"It sure ain't no Taj Mahal."

"Couldn't be avoided," I said professionally, echoing my father. "You ordered the wrong stone. Alabaster quartz is for tombstones. It's not suited for walls. Too heavy, too hard to maneuver. All things considered, we did a remarkable job."

His fat eyes fell upon me.

"You can say that again."

"That smokehouse will outlast these mountains. If you'd asked for the Acropolis the old man would have built it. You wanted a smokehouse and that's precisely what you got."

Big as a walrus he was, shrugging his silken shoulders, not putting up an argument. Then he suddenly blurted it out:

"Looks like a shithouse to me."

He pulled a wallet from inside his coat pocket, removed a check, and handed it to me.

"Give it to Nick. Paid in full."

The check confused me. Everything about it seemed wrong. It was written in the amount of fifteen hundred dollars, but not to my father. On the contrary, my father had written the check payable to Sam Ramponi on the Reno Bank and Trust Company. I racked my head trying to make some sense out of the transaction.

"What in the hell's this?" I asked.

"It's your old man's IOU from the poker game."

I laughed. "Absurd. My father hasn't got fifteen hundred. He hasn't got fifteen cents. He hasn't had a bank account for years, and he's *never* had a bank account in Reno."

Sam touched the check with his thick finger. "Isn't that your father's signature?"

"The one he uses when he's drunk, yes."

"Drunk or sober, it's legal tender."

"It's not legal and it's not tender. It's just a bad check."

He turned his palms in a shrug.

"So he wrote a bad check. That's against the law. I don't want to make trouble, Tony. Me and your father, we go back a long ways. He owes me fifteen hundred from the poker game and I owe him for that thing out there. So," he smiled with blameless eyes, "we're even."

He had us, my father and me. Euchred. It was staggering. My God, how long had I been tumbling around in this nightmare? Dragged from the peace and quiet of my home by the sea, tricked into becoming a stonemason's helper, hauled off into the mountains with three tosspots, to spend six wretched days building a hunchbacked monstrosity?

Oh, the pain! The blisters! The screaming backache, the tortured feet, the dead weight of those stones, the delirium of our exhaustion, our wraithlike deaths! How long, O Lord, how long? Why was I being punished so? I scanned the past. Was it the waitress in Paris? The three Naples hookers? I have paid, O Lord, I have paid and paid like a credit card that revolves and revolves. Close the account, O Lord. Give me a break. Give me peace. I am wiser, I have learned my lesson. There shall be no more transgressions. I shall return to the church, for I am old now, too fucking old.

Ramponi, my tormentor, crook, card cheat. Rage. I lunged at him through the car window, my fingers around his thick neck, my mind searching for cruel, obscene curses — something better than motherfucker. But the fat man, like most fat men, was quicker than a bird, twisting from my grasp, and the best I could get off was, "All right for you, Sam Ramponi! You'll be sorry!"

He stepped on the gas and the car moved fifty feet to the motel office and stopped. I wasn't through. I pursued him, walking grimly as he got out of his Cadillac, ready for my onslaught, waiting, fists doubled, big as a walrus, prepared to fight.

Maybe he could have taken me, maybe not. He was ponderous as a hippo, fat, a pasta man. I was short, runty, and strong as an ox. I had been preparing for this without knowing it. Six days on the rock pile. I was like iron. He was older, over seventy. I was a youth of fifty. He had no chance. Quickness was on my side. A generation separated us.

I took my stance, fists raised. I spoke:

"You cheated my father, Ramponi. Now you have to reckon with his son."

He brought up his fists.

"I didn't cheat. When you play cards with your old man you don't have to cheat. There's no way you can lose."

"You take him for fifteen hundred, and you don't call that cheating?"

"It was three thousand, Tony. I settled for half."

"Who changed the stakes? When I left you were playing for nickels and dimes."

"Your father raised the stakes. He wanted action. He said he'd quit unless we made it a no-limit game."

"You jerk! The man was drunk."

"He was no drunker'n me. We were all drunk."

Then silence. Cold statues we were, facing one another, Greeks in stone. Staring, fearful of movement. Who would strike first — the crucial blow, the first? We began to circle, slowly round and round. It became tedious. Then it became clear. We didn't want to fight. We had one thing in common: cowardice.

But Sam was first to back off. Dropping his hands, he groaned, turned his back, and stepped into the motel office. It gave me a sense of victory. As he disappeared, I put my hands on my hips and sneered. I felt pretty good walking back to our cabin.

The old man was taking a shower. I pulled the phony check from my pocket and studied it. The dilemma was, should I give it to him, or would it be better if I pretended not to know? Besides, it was really none of my business. It was a private transaction, a gambling debt between him and Sam. I should not have accepted the check in the first place. Then a way out occurred to me. I took an envelope from the motel stationery, slipped the check inside, and sealed it. Presently he emerged naked from the bathroom and scrambled quickly into bed.

I handed him the envelope.

"Sam said to give you this."

He sat up and looked at it. The fact that it was sealed reassured him and he tore it open. His lips broke into a false smile as he examined the check.

"Been a long time since I had a real good paycheck," he said.

20

THUNDER AND lightning wakened me. The slant roof rumbled as the rain buried it. The wind howled. The cabin creaked. Someone pounded at the door. It was Sam Ramponi, shouting, "Open up, open up!"

I stumbled out of bed and opened the door. Rain rushed in like an assassin. Ramponi and his wife stood in the deluge, he in a white plastic raincoat blowing up around his face and she in a red one. He shone a large flashlight in my face.

"Where's Nick?" he yelled.

"Asleep."

"Get him up. We got big trouble."

He rushed away, the flashlight beam spearing sheets of rain as he struggled to pull the raincoat away from his face. Birdlike, Mrs. Ramponi followed, hopping over rain puddles as they ran in the direction of the smokehouse.

I drew on my pants and shook my father, shouting, pulling off the bed covers. He shivered, naked and quivering, and squeezed himself into a fetal ball and refused to waken to the clamor around him. I left him that way, in the path of the marauding rain. He floundered, wet and asleep, as I pulled on a windbreaker and dashed out into the black, thundering night.

Toward the smokehouse I ran, the rain peppering my face and slapping my body with water bullets, gleeful and shrieking with delight, telling me the smokehouse was down in the storm, down, down, down. I laughed with joy. I hoped it was true. The monster was down, it had to be down. And it was. Down. All the way, flat on its ass, down.

It lay sprawled, dead in the rain, a pile of bones, a Godzilla breathing its last — the walls collapsed, washed out at the foundations, rain beating it unmercifully, thunder exploding boom boom, lightning flashing zip zip, lighting up the forest as bright as the sun.

Holding hands, the Ramponis stood beside the fallen ogre with bowed heads, paying their last respects. I went to Mrs. Ramponi's side. Her face was saddened in disappointment, her eyes moist at the loss of her beloved smokehouse and all that it had promised. There was no way to conceal my delight. I took her hand and squeezed it, and when she turned to me I smiled, and she could see the demons dancing in my eyes.

''Too bad,'' I smiled. ''What a shame.''

Ramponi speared the ruin with his flashlight and I caught sight of a number of troublesome stones that we had had to fight in order to set them in the wall. Fallen enemies now, heaped on the battlefield, a Waterloo of rocks, grotesque in the falling rain.

''Hell of a mess,'' Ramponi breathed. ''Ah, well, I guess it's for the best. It was a terrible eyesore. Ruined the property.''

He took his wife's arm and they slogged off in the rain. Turning, she looked back at the devastation. It reminded me of Lot's wife.

''Tell Nick I'll see him in the morning,'' Ramponi called.

Back at the cabin I found Nick Molise sound asleep under a pile of blankets. Even his head was buried. But he had risen during the excitement, for a fresh jug stood at the bedside table, the last jug from the purchase Ramponi had supplied.

21

IN THE MORNING the storm was gone and so was my father. I checked the jug. Down another pint. I dressed and stepped outside. The rain had washed the giant forest, settled the dust, cleared the air, and changed the world. Birds shrieked and chipmunks with plumed tails leaped from branch to branch like circus aerialists. The whole earth had put on its Sunday best to celebrate the smokehouse fiasco. The news must have reached far into the sky, for curious clouds drifted past, surveying the ruins.

Angry voices came from the smokehouse area. I hurried over. My father stood in the rubble, hurling aside small stones, trying to clear away the glut of debris. Sam Ramponi was yelling at him. He was in his black silk work clothes and chewing a cigar.

"Don't be a horse's ass," he was saying. "Quit while you're ahead."

"I ain't ahead!" my father yelled, heaving a stone. "I'm behind."

"What's the trouble?" I said.

"Damn fool wants to start over." Then to my father: "Quit, you dumb son of a bitch! Get your stuff together and I'll drive you home!"

Old Nick went right on heaving stones. His bleary eyes showed him a very tired man.

"What's the deal?" I asked.

"No deal. We do it right, that's all."

Ramponi screamed: "I don't want it right and I don't want it wrong! I don't want it period. I never wanted a smokehouse. It was my wife's idea. I hate deer meat. I hate beef. I hate pork. I like chicken, and I like fish. So leave it alone. Ruined. Don't touch it! Pack up your gear and I'll drive you back."

"No, sir," Papa said. "We're staying right here. We'll build it again, if it takes all winter." Pooped, he eased himself upon a flat stone.

Let them argue, let them destroy one another; I was through. I would do no more. I left them hollering and walked back to the cabin. I took a shower. I packed our clothes. I read an old paperback. Occasionally I went to the open door and put my ear toward the smokehouse, invisible through the trees. I heard nothing. But I knew he was there, the jug on his knees. I told myself I was doing the right thing, and yet I was troubled and wondering if I were wrong in not helping him.

Around noon Mrs. Ramponi rushed up to the door.

"There's something wrong with your father."

She ran toward the forest and I followed. Nick lay on his back beside the creek, his face to the sky, eyes closed, his breathing deep and difficult. I dropped to his side and he opened his eyes and moaned. Mrs. Ramponi sank to her haunches and touched his flushed face.

"Heart attack," she said flatly. "I've seen it before. My own father."

"How about just plain drunk? I've seen that before too."

"Let's try artificial respiration."

She got to her knees beside him, took a deep breath, and

pressed her mouth to his, pushing her breath down his throat. It wakened him with a start. He opened his eyes, saw her face, and loosed a cry of protest, fighting her off. She grasped his head firmly and tried again.

"No!" he growled. "Leave me alone, goddamnit!"

I scooped water from the stream and dashed it into his face. He licked the water from his lips.

Mrs. Ramponi got to her feet.

"The man's dying."

"The man's drunk."

"Don't move him. I'll get a blanket. We've got to keep him warm."

She dashed away. I pulled him to a sitting position, but he was as limp as a string, his head flopping. Hoisting him to my shoulder I expected a great heaviness, but he was alarmingly light, no heavier than a sack of toys as I carried him toward the motel. Mrs. Ramponi saw us coming and became very agitated.

"Put him down, man. You're killing him!"

I carried him past her into the office and lowered him upon a leather couch. She covered him with a light blanket and went for his mouth again with artificial respiration. He gagged and twisted and grimaced and pushed her away.

"Water," he said.

Water? Incredible. He rarely drank water. He had to be very sick indeed. Mrs. Ramponi brought him a glassful from the kitchen and held it to his lips, and he sucked it down greedily.

"More."

He drank two glassfuls more and sank into a deep sleep. His face was hot and dry against my fingers. He was not drunk. He seemed very tired and flaccid, overcome with weariness. Mumbling, he opened his eyes and tried to rise.

"Water closet . . ."

He threw off the blanket and stood up, swaying. I steadied him through the kitchen to the bathroom and he stood before the bowl, asleep and rocking. As I steered him back to the office he veered toward the kitchen sink.

"Water."

He drank three glassfuls, then returned to the bathroom. I held him erect with my arms around his waist. It was the same interminable business. Finally he was on the leather sofa again, confused by a sinister lethargy, his breathing loud.

Watching, Mrs. Ramponi said, "You know what I think? Cancer of the bladder. My uncle had it. We better call an ambulance. I don't want him dying here." She pushed the desk phone toward me. "Tahoe Ambulance Service." She gave me the number.

Dialing the operator, I asked for Dr. Frank Maselli in San Elmo. For more than forty years my father had been Maselli's reluctant patient, avoiding him as much as possible, for he had but one unvarying prescription for my father's good health: stop drinking.

Maselli's first question over the phone was: "Is he drunk?"

I said he was not drunk, and as I began to explain my father's condition Dr. Maselli cut me off.

"Is he thirsty?"

"Very."

"I hope you're not giving him wine."

"Just water."

"Does he piss a lot?"

"Gallons."

"Smell his breath."

"What?"

"Smell your father's breath."

I put the phone down, bent over my old man, and sniffed his heavy breathing.

"Smells sweet," I said into the phone.

"So it finally happened."

"What, Doc?"

"Where are you?"

I told him.

"How far from Auburn?"

"About fifty miles."

"Get him to the Auburn Hospital as fast as you can. I'll meet you there." He hung up. I turned to Mrs. Ramponi.

"Can you drive us to the Auburn Hospital?"

"Lord God, yes."

22

It was a diabetic coma.

He had drifted into it slowly over a period of days and it was five hours before Dr. Maselli and a staff physician at the Auburn Hospital could raise him from the abyss of coma and back to consciousness. They purged his bloodstream with intravenous saltwater and infused him with insulin. He had a severe reaction to the insulin, going into shock, and they had to counter with sucrose. The sucrose shot up his blood sugar and they injected insulin again, this time in smaller amounts, until his sugar level was more or less stabilized. Meanwhile I waited in the reception room at Auburn Hospital, watching an angry sun go down.

About eight that night Dr. Maselli walked in. He was small, fat, cherubic and seventy-three; a textbook medic, a good family doctor, with the rosy cheeks of an Angelo Musso boy. He always managed to look cheerful and concerned, but he was actually a cold professional who gave out as little information as possible.

He liked being mysterious. When he took your temperature or your blood pressure he never gave you the numbers. He had treated the Molise family for many years now — their broken bones, measles, mumps, strep infections, clap, colic, influenza, Mama's gall bladder, her backaches and her bizarre female disorders. From time to time he massaged my writhing father's prostate and prescribed pills for unstated ailments. My father liked Maselli not for his healing technique but because he told my mother nothing. One thing was certain: Maselli knew more about my father than anybody in the world.

"How is he?"

Maselli flopped into a leather chair.

"He's out of danger now. The rest is up to him."

He bit off the end of a cigar and told me what had been done to lift him out of the coma.

"He's going to be okay, then?"

"Hardly." He lit the cigar. "Your father's an alcoholic, you know. A diabetic alcoholic." That seemed to amuse him. "How's that for a dichotomy?"

"I didn't know about the diabetes."

"A borderline case for years. I kept warning him but he refused treatment. I finally got him on Orinase — that's a pill, you know — but nothing helps if you're smashed all the time."

"What about now?"

"Insulin."

"And cut down on the wine," I said.

"Cut down, hell. He's got to quit cold turkey. After all, wine is nothing more than grape sugar. Deadly. He'll have to restrict his pasta too, and bread. He eats too much bread anyway."

"He'll make it, Doc." I said it routinely, the usual cliché.

"I'm not so sure. Your father's will to die is much stronger than his will to live."

"Wrong, Doc," I insisted, the cliché again. "He's got tremendous will power. You should have seen the way he hung in there, finishing that smokehouse."

Maselli frowned thoughtfully.

"That smokehouse business troubles me. I mean, the way you

say he botched it. Your father never built a crooked wall in his life."

"He was sick, worn out."

"He's been sick and worn out and a borderline diabetic for years, but he always delivered, always did a good job. But this last one . . . I don't know. Strange business."

I remembered the IOU to Ramponi, the way it must have humiliated the old man, but I didn't mention it to the doctor, who suddenly opened up a spider's nest of facts about my father's health that left me stunned. Nick Molise had severe high blood pressure. His heart suffered from myocardial insufficiency. His liver was enlarged and malfunctioning. His kidneys had undergone cystic degeneration. He had a chronic bladder infection. His eyes indicated the onset of cataracts. And now, diabetes . . .

Having said it all, Maselli seemed relieved, as if it should have been said a long time ago, as if shifting responsibility and disclaiming any guilt for the crumbling ruin. It left me depressed and I felt a tightening in my chest as I went to the window and watched the heavy night settling down, the dark trees on the hospital grounds, the slow-moving traffic in the foggy street beyond. Maselli bothered me. Why did he have to tell everything? He had kept silent all these years, now he was copping out. Why did I have to suffer too?

"A matter of survival," he said vaguely.

"I'd like to see my father now."

"He's been sedated. Come back tomorrow."

I walked out, down the stairs to the front office and outside, dreading the grim business ahead, my mother, her lamentations, her tears. Riding the bus back to San Elmo I considered not getting off, rolling right through that depressing town to the Sacramento airport and a flight home.

How long had I been away now? Was it a month, a year? What had happened to my love for writing, the urgency of it? I groveled in self-pity. My father lay in the hospital, a dying man, and all I felt was a tragic compassion for myself. I was back at the Toyo Fish Company shoveling fertilizer, unloading trucks, I was at the Holy Ghost Mission eating bread and stew, I was in the Lincoln Heights Jail on a vagrancy charge. I was scum again, proletarian scum, the son of an ill-fated mason who had struggled all his life for a bit of space on earth. Like father, like son. Ah, Dostoyevsky! Fyodor could have come walking out of the fog and placed his hand on my shoulder and it would have meant nothing. How could a man live without his father? How could he wake up in the morning and say to himself: my father is gone forever?

23

THE LIGHTS were out and my mother's house was in darkness as I turned into the yard, but I saw that the front door was open and I heard the creak of the rocker on the front porch, then my mother's voice:

"Is he dead?"

There was no anxiety in her voice, no emotion, only a flat acceptance of what had to be.

"No, Mama. I just came from the hospital."

"How is he?"

"Okay," I said, finding a bit of her face in the darkness. "Dr. Maselli's with him." I sat on the top porch stair and leaned against the post.

"It's been coming," she said. "I've known all along. Is it his heart?"

"He's got diabetes."

She rose and kissed a white rosary in her hand.

"His father died of diabetes."

"How old was he?"

"Young. Only eighty. When can we go see him?"

"Maybe tomorrow."

"Are you hungry? I made a meat loaf."

I followed her into the house. The meat loaf was in the open oven. It didn't look appetizing, as if it had been prepared for my father, his supper, and I could not eat it. As I spread peanut butter on a slice of bread my mother came to the door. She was in a gray and blue dress with a black shawl over her hair.

"I'm going to church."

"At this hour? It's closed."

"Not anymore. Father Martin keeps the doors open all night."

"Go in the morning."

"Now. I want to pray."

"I'll call a cab."

"No. I'd like to walk."

She left and I felt the peanut butter sticking to my mouth, and I thought of her walking seven blocks in the night, across the railroad tracks, past the lumberyard and out Pacific Street to the frame church in the Mexican neighborhood. I went after her.

As I caught up with her and fell in step she did not acknowledge I was there, moving instead with other thoughts and quiet determination. How beautiful she seemed in that warm night along a dimly lit street of rundown houses, loving that tyrant husband in the hospital, her face like a dove, sweetly moving, reminding me of an old photograph of her in a large hat at Capitol Park in Sacramento when she was twenty, leaning against a tree and smiling, so precious then, so precious now that I wanted to take her into my arms like a lover and carry her through the church door.

Though it was nearly midnight the church was not deserted. It reminded me of an Italian proverb: "If you see a crowd of women, the church is close at hand." A dozen women knelt in the pews, all wearing shawls, old like my mother, most in prayer before the Virgin's altar. My mother stayed at the back of the church, entering a pew and kneeling to kiss the cross on her rosary. I knelt beside her and listened to the old wooden edifice crack and wheeze after the heat of the day. There was a smell of layers and layers of incense and fresh flowers, like marriages piled on funerals, and leaping shadows on the walls behind tiers of vigil lights.

Peace smoothed my mother's face. She had not been married in this church, but her children had been baptized there and educated by the nuns of this parish. Her faith was nourishing her now, and from the way her lips moved you could see her sucking up the magic of the place.

After an hour of kneeling beside her my bones ached and I sat back with folded hands. Presently she sat back too, the beads in her hands. I was very tired now, and sleepy, and I stretched out on the pew and closed my eyes. Her fingers stroked my hair and she drew my head into her lap and smiled down at me. The beads danced over my eyes as I fell asleep. We were there through the night, starting back to the house in the new day, along streets that asked about my father and why he was not with us.

24

AFTER BREAKFAST I telephoned Virgil and told him that the old man was in the Auburn Hospital. Without giving me a chance to elaborate he asked, "Is he drunk?"

"He's not drunk. He's sick."

"How much is it going to cost?"

"He's very sick with diabetes. He was in a coma for five hours."

"Diabetes?" He was relieved. "That's not so bad. He's on Medicare, you know."

"He almost died."

"So what? He's alive, isn't he?"

"Barely."

After a silence: "Gee."

I told him Mama was having dinner for the immediate family at six and she wanted him there with the others. Afterward we would drive up to the Auburn Hospital and pay the old man a visit.

"Can't make it," he said. "This is my bowling night."

"Don't be a jerk," I said. "For once let's do something as a family. We owe it to Papa. You're his favorite, Virge. I guess you know that.''

It made him cackle.

''That's very funny, Henry, specially since his dislike for us is evenly divided.''

''Will you come?''

''What's Mama cooking?''

''What's the difference. This isn't a celebration, it's a solemn moment.''

''Veal with peppers, and I'll show up.''

''You got it.''

Trying to contact my brother Mario was beset with the usual complications. Kids hollered in the background, and the television was on full blast. My sister-in-law answered.

''Hello, Peggy. Is Mario there?''

''He's asleep. You still around?''

''Will you wake him, please. It's important.''

''What keeps you in San Elmo, Henry? Don't tell me you're writing a sex novel about your father and mother.''

''Peggy, listen. Papa's in the hospital.''

''So he got flattened again. Good.''

''He's very sick with diabetes.''

''Really? My aunt had diabetes. He'll be okay. Just give him plenty of orange juice.''

''Great idea, Peggy. I'll tell Dr. Maselli. Will you please call Mario to the phone?''

That was it. End of conversation. She left the phone off the hook and completely forgot me. For twenty minutes I sat by the telephone waiting, listening to children squalling, doors opening, dogs barking. I heard Peggy spanking the little girl's ass, and the child's shrieks. Then the fall of furniture and the wails of the boy. I heard Mario cursing and demanding his breakfast. He must have kicked the dog, for it yelped in pain. A brawl ensued, man and wife in combat, the thud of bodies, the breaking of dishes, the screams of children, the wild barking of dogs, the sputter of a truck engine, the howl of burning rubber, the clatter of the truck bed as the car ground its gears and spun off.

An hour later I reached Mario at the railroad dispatch office.

"When are we going to get together?" he asked.

I told him about Papa.

"Jesus," he said. "That's awful. At his age, too. Diabetes . . . what's diabetes? Isn't it some kind of venereal disease?"

"Nothing like that, you dope. It's an excess of sugar in the blood and urine."

"That's right. I knew it had something to do with urine. Where did he contact it?"

"You don't contact it because it's not contagious."

"That's funny. Papa hates sugar."

"He's better now. We're going to the hospital tonight, all of us, and that includes you. Mama wants you at the house for dinner at six. Okay?"

"I'll come to dinner, but not the hospital. Old Nick hates my guts. I'll only upset him."

"You're wrong, man, dead wrong. Papa *likes* you. He told me so just the other day. You're his favorite. Of all of us you're the only one who tried to learn his trade. Me and Virgil gave up, but you were loyal, Mario, a good son. You did your best. You failed, but that's not the point. You tried. He remembers that. He thinks you've still got the makings of a great bricklayer. He may not show it— you know how he is— but he's crazy about you, Mario. He respects you. He barely tolerates me, and he doesn't like Virgil at all. But you're the apple of his eye."

His voice softened.

"I like him too, damn it. Always have. Maybe we've had some battles, but I don't hold it against him."

"Good for you, Mario. Forget the past. Come to the hospital with us. He's an old man now. He may die any day. So make peace with him. Have a clear conscience. Let him know you love him as much as he loves you."

"I will, Henry. Maybe I could bring him something. How about a jug of Angelo Musso?"

"He can't have any wine."

"How about flowers. A plant."

"Maybe."

"Maybe bedroom slippers."

"Perfect."

"And a robe."

"Fine."

"See you at Mama's."

Suddenly I realized he was putting me on — and himself — that he had no intention of coming to dinner, or of buying his father a gift, or of visiting him in the hospital, for Mario was a dreamer who never followed through on his good intentions.

25

WE WAITED for him at dinner, seated around the kitchen table, Stella, Virgil and I, sipping wine, crunching slivers of carrots and celery while my mother brooded over her stove, tending the main dish, which was tripe, *trippa Milanese,* something plain and austere, in keeping with the grim occasion. She had set a place at the head of the table for her husband, a sort of homage to him, and his absence was heavy in the air.

At six-thirty she walked out on the front porch to look for her wayward son. With folded arms she looked up and down the street before returning to the kitchen.

"We eat," she announced.

The *trippa Milanese* was neither plain nor austere, it was wild and ravishing, squares of honeycomb tripe prepared with rice, bell peppers and tomato sauce, sprinkled with Parmesan cheese and seasoned with butter and spices.

Virgil forgot his wish for veal and peppers and ate like a famished dog, swiftly clearing his plate and demanding more, a glutton at a feast rather than a concerned son about to visit his ailing father. He finished off with a vulgar belch, gulped down wine, and announced that the time had come to face reality, the facts of life.

"Let's take things in their proper perspective," he said like the president of the Bank of America. "First, there's the matter of our father's insurance. Have any of you thought about it lately? Is it in order? Has anyone read the fine print?"

Stella flung down her napkin.

"Shut up, Virgil!"

He stared innocently.

"Have I offended someone? Am I not permitted a simple inquiry? In the banking business the approach is direct and to the point. Sentiment is ruled out."

"Papa isn't dead," Stella said. "He's sick."

"You can't run and hide from these problems." Virgil smiled condescendingly. "Face them courageously, honestly: insurance, funeral costs, Mama's future . . ."

He might as well have punched his mother in the stomach. She got to her feet and staggered from the room. We heard her sob as she closed the bedroom door. Virgil shook his head doubtfully.

"Nice going," I said.

Stella snatched up a slice of bread and flung it into his face. "You're a beast!" she said. "You always were. I hate you!"

He stared at his fingers as we sat there listening to Mama opening drawers and moving about in the bedroom. She came out dressed for the visit to the hospital. There was too much powder on her face and she was draped in that disreputable whorehouse coat of Aunt Carmelina's. Dangling from her arm was a huge black patent leather purse.

"I'm ready," she said.

"Must you wear that awful coat?" Stella complained.

"I like that coat," Virgil said, trying to make amends. "It looks nice on you."

"It's cheap," Stella said. She glanced at Mama's feet. "Look at your stockings, all wrinkled."

Reaching beneath her coat and brown satin dress, Mama hitched up both stockings with one motion.

"There."

"Oh, God," Stella said.

She brought Mama to the light of the window, moistened a napkin with spittle, and dabbed away heavy blotches of face powder under Mama's eyes and around her neck.

"Try to look nice, for Papa's sake."

"He don't care," Mama said crossly.

We walked out to Stella's Pontiac. Mama and Virgil got in the back seat and I sat up front with Stella. It was twenty miles to the Auburn Hospital. As Stella started the car my mother said, "Wait. I forgot to leave a note for Mario."

"What for?" Virgil said.

"To meet us at the hospital."

"Forget it. He won't show up."

"He might," Mama said, groping about, having difficulty getting out of the car.

"I'll do it," I said, stepping out.

"Put the note in the refrigerator," Mama said. "He'll look for it there."

I went to the kitchen, scribbled the note, and placed it atop a freshly baked apple cobbler in the refrigerator.

Then we drove to the hospital.

26

Two by two we trooped past the reception desk and down the glossy hospital corridor, Mama and Virgil, Stella and I. At the door to my father's room we paused for a consultation. Mama was a little breathless. The powder had vanished from her flushed face and she pushed the fur collar away from her hot neck.

"How do I look?"

"You'd look a lot better if you took off that damned coat," Stella said, reaching out to strip it from Mama's shoulders. "I'll carry it for you."

Mama relented and Stella bundled the coat in her arms. The brown satin dress beneath the coat looked shabby and wrinkled, as if it might have come from the Salvation Army or the nineteenth century. There were places where her underwear bulged and the dress hung crookedly, the hem on the bias.

"Pull up your stockings," Harriet said.

"Oh, he doesn't bother with things like that anymore," Mama said, but she nevertheless gave her stockings a hitch. All of us examined her critically. Poor Mama. Even Dior could not have improved matters. It was the way she stood there, kinda bow-legged, in somebody else's dress and falling-down stockings and shoes that looked too big.

"Ready?" I said, reaching for the door handle.

Stella gave Mama a reassuring hug.

"Stay cool now. Don't cry."

That started the tears immediately, but she choked them off as we entered the room. Nick sat up on the high hospital bed, serene, almost languid. We gathered around him, saying hello and touching him. He looked splendid, clean-shaven, hair trimmed and combed, mustache clipped, fresh and rested, not sick at all. Mama gazed at him and wilted like warm butter, her eyes filling. She bent down and kissed him, and so did Stella. A strong aroma of shaving lotion wafted from him.

"Where's Mario?" he asked.

"He had to work," I said.

"Still mad at me about that baseball business."

"Not so," Stella said. "Mario has a family now. He's forgotten all about it."

"Not Mario. He don't forget anything."

Mama squeezed his hand.

"Do they treat you good?"

"Real good."

I had never seen him so composed, at such ease. Maybe it was the Valium.

"You look thin," Mama said. "Do you get enough to eat?"

"Plenty to eat. Asparagus with toast for supper. String beans and Jell-O."

"Jell-O? You won't eat Jell-O."

"Tasted good."

"What kind of sauce on the asparagus?"

"No sauce."

Mama was appalled.

"What kind of a place is this?"

"Nice place. Nurses, nice."

"You look pale." She turned to us. "Don't you think he looks pale?"

We didn't think so.

"I feel good," he said. Then, pleased: "I take insulin now."

I asked if he gave the injection to himself.

"Miss Quinlan gave it to me."

"That'll be your job from now on, Mama," Stella said.

"Every day, from now on," Papa said. "Talk to Miss Quinlan. She'll show you what to do."

"Who's Miss Quinlan?" Mama said.

"My nurse," Papa said.

It bothered Mama. She folded her arms.

"Lots to learn," he went on. "What I eat, what I can't eat. Not like the old days. No more pasta. Not much, anyway."

Mama was astonished. "No pasta . . . no spaghetti?"

"A little bit. Once a week."

"Lasagne?"

"Christmas and Easter."

"Pastina? The little ones, in garlic and oil?"

"Talk to Miss Quinlan. She's got a list."

"I'll talk to Dr. Maselli. I don't need to talk to a nurse."

Virgil had a gift for him, a pack of Italian stogies. He took the pack tentatively, then passed it back. "I don't smoke no more, son. I quit for good."

"I don't believe it," Virgil said.

"Doctor's orders. No more wine, no more cigars."

"And no pasta?" Stella smiled doubtfully. "It won't be easy, Papa."

His eyes shone.

"I'll make it."

Mama clasped his wrist. "Course you will. First, get out of this place. Come home. Rest a few days, until you feel good. No more work, no more mountains. Sleep in your own bed. Go downtown, walk around. Talk to the menfolks at the Roma. Maybe one cigar after supper. Pretty soon you'll feel better. I don't care what the doctor says: one cigar never hurt anybody. Same with a little spaghetti, and a glass of wine. You ain't gonna live forever, so enjoy it while you can. I'll talk to Dr. Maselli. He understands."

It made the old man smile.

"We'll see."

A preposterous dilemma. I didn't think much of his chances. Sixty-five years of wine and pasta and cigars, and now he proposed changing to a life of self-denial. How could he resist the siren fragrances wafted from his wife's cauldrons? Every room in his house was scented with the good life, the Mediterranean life. I looked down at him in that stark hospital gown, eyes bright with the determination to stay alive, his jaw as square as a stone, fists in his lap, this strong, decaying man, all shot to hell on the inside, who now proposed to pit himself against the tender guile of a woman who had kept him vigorous and content through the thousands of days of his existence. Yet, in spite of everything, miracles did happen. A man could change, if only to survive.

A nurse entered the room. She was around forty, a bleached blonde, tall, attractive, cheerful, chatty, and carrying a specimen jar.

"Good evening all!" she greeted, and we fumbled out of her way as she moved to the bedside.

"And how's my naughty boy tonight?"

"Purty good," Papa grinned.

She fluffed his pillow, bending over him with hefty breasts in a tight uniform, tucking him in, brushing back his hair, embarrassing him as he avoided Mama's cold glare.

"This is my family," he said.

"How are you all?" the nurse said. "I'm Miss Quinlan. Doesn't he look fine tonight? You should have seen him *last* night! It only goes to show what loving care can do. Such a good boy. Not a bit of trouble.''

"When can we take him home?''

"That's for the doctor to decide.''

She held out the specimen jar to Papa.

"Have you got a bit of something for me, Daddy?''

Daddy!

You could see my mother writhe as she tried to destroy Miss Quinlan with a sneer while the nurse helped Papa out of bed and toward the bathroom, his gown open and flapping in back, his bare ass showing.

He entered, closed the door, bolted it carefully, then reappeared with the half-filled jar.

"What a lovely specimen!'' Nurse Quinlan enthused, holding the bottle up to the light. "Clear as honey, the best so far.''

Nick cowered back into bed past Mama's smoldering eyes, covering himself to the chin, as if to hide his body. Miss Quinlan fussed with his pillow, smoothed his blankets, pushed back his hair.

"Good night, sweetie,'' she whispered, marching off with the specimen.

A gaping silence filled the space vacated by Miss Quinlan. Mama looked lost, etherized, a shambles. She glanced toward the door, as if Miss Quinlan were still there.

"Puttana!'' she said.

The bell rang, signaling the end of the visiting hour. "Time to go,'' Virgil said.

Mama bent to kiss her husband on the forehead, searching deeply into his eyes.

"Be careful,'' she warned.

Stella kissed him and Virgil and I said good night. We left, looking back at him watching us, a lonely old man in a stark room, on a high bed, filtered, obfuscated, blended into a blue wall.

Down the corridor in a fast shuffle raced my mother, anxious to put the hospital behind her. Stella and Virgil quickened their steps to keep up but I hung back, intrigued by images on a television screen inside one of the hospital rooms. It was a baseball game. Sitting up in bed, a man watched.

"Who's playing?" I asked.

"The Giants and the Dodgers."

It explained what had happened to Mario.

27

THREE NIGHTS later I dreamed of my father's funeral. Miss Quinlan was at the graveside across from Mario, and they were smiling intimately. Nearby was a hearse drawn by four black horses adorned with silver harnesses and white plumes. My wife and sons were in the driver's seat, smirking at my mother as she spaded earth into the grave, and a score of mourners chatted and laughed without reverence, like revelers at a picnic. I was only an observer, but my presence was not in the dream. I was sodden with the residual effect as I wakened at ten o'clock and walked into the kitchen and poured coffee. Through the window I saw my mother in the backyard, throwing grain to her chickens. The phone rang.

It was Dr. Maselli calling from the hospital.

"Have you seen your father this morning?"

"He's in the hospital."

"Not anymore. I just came from his room. His clothes are gone and so is he."

I laughed. "How long has he been gone?"

"He left between seven and eight this morning."

I laughed again.

"What the hell's so funny?" the doctor said. "The old cocker hasn't had his insulin this morning."

"Is that bad?"

"If he stops to gas up in some saloon it could be another coma."

"Maybe he's on a bus back to San Elmo."

"Better check and see. Try the Onyx and the Café Roma."

I asked if he had tried any of the saloons near the hospital.

"I've got patients here. I can't leave now."

"How about the police?"

"What for? He's not a criminal, he's just a goddamn fool."

"What do I do if I find him?"

"If he's in San Elmo, get him to my office. I'll be there in an hour. Or put him in a car and bring him back to the hospital."

I dressed quickly and slipped out of the house and into the cool and lucid morning, fresh upon my skin.

My old man! What a treasure he was, what excitement he kicked up! That was his genius, a talent for shaking up the small world in which he lived. I walked quickly toward town, laughing quietly, so pleased with him. He might die, but what of that? Dostoyevsky was dead, yet very much alive in my heart. He had come to me like the grace of God, a flash of lightning that illumined my life. My father had that same iridescence, a nimbus around me, my own flesh and blood, a poet asserting his will to live.

I stopped at the Onyx Bar first. Art Pinto was behind the counter, serving beer to a couple of brakemen. I asked if he had seen my father.

"Not anymore, Henry. He ain't allowed."

The Café Roma was deserted except for Frank Mascarini, polishing glasses behind the bar. He had not seen my father in days.

I asked, "Where's Zarlingo this morning, and Lou Cavallaro?"

"They don't get here till noon."

I walked out. The day was warming up. Standing in the shade under the awning of the Leroy Hotel, I pondered the problem. Where would a man leaving the Auburn Hospital find a drink? Obviously, the nearest saloon. That had been my hunch in the first place. He wouldn't waste time waiting for a bus to take him back to his hometown if he was in flight from the hospital. Chances were he'd duck into the first saloon in sight. He had to be in Auburn somewhere, in a saloon on Chop Suey Street not far from the hospital. I walked up the street to the Hertz people and rented a Chevy for the drive to Auburn.

Chop Suey Street was a block long, the Chinese section of Auburn. It consisted of six saloons squeezed among the crumbling frame and brick buildings. I parked at the end of the old, elm-lined block and entered an establishment called the Silverado. It was cool and dark inside and fragrant with the vapors of beer. The young bartender paid no attention to me.

"I'm looking for my father," I explained. "Old guy, about my size. Seventy-six years old, wearing khaki pants and shirt. Has a mustache."

He nodded toward the dark interior.

"Take your pick. We got several answering that description."

Back in the gloom I walked among the tables where a dozen old guys sat in somnolent silence, sipping beer and sherry. It surprised me how much they all looked like my father, the same gnarled hands, the same scuffed, turned-up shoes, the same battered hats, the same opaque eyes staring into nowhere. Nick was not among them, nor was he in any of the other bars along the street.

I walked back to the rented car and drove a few blocks to the Auburn downtown area. He wasn't in the bus depot, and the cocktail lounges along the main street were too fancy for his taste and I didn't stop to look for him there. Instead I drove to the hospital, wondering doubtfully whether he had returned.

Miss Quinlan and another nurse were at the desk on the second floor as I stepped from the elevator. Miss Quinlan was talking into the phone. She was startled to see me.

"It's your father," she said, handing me the phone.

I took the phone.

"Hello, Papa. Where are you?"

He hung up.

I cradled the phone and asked Miss Quinlan if she knew where my father had called from.

"Some place on the highway. A winery."

"The Angelo Musso winery?"

"That's the place."

"How did he sound?"

"I think he's been drinking."

"Does he need help?"

"Without insulin he's in desperate need of help."

"Why did he call, Miss Quinlan? What did he want?"

She hesitated. "He asked me to come out there and meet him."

"What for?"

"He wanted to show me the vineyard." It made her smile. "The old rascal . . ."

I spun around and started to leave, but what she had said troubled me, and I turned back and drew her away from the desk and the other nurse standing there.

"Miss Quinlan," I said. "That 'old rascal' remark, what did you mean by it?"

She studied me with wide sky-blue eyes, carefully sorting out her answer: "Last winter I had a patient on a kidney machine, a fine old gentleman, ninety-two years old. The dear man died in my arms, with his hand in my panties. You know what I mean, Mr. Molise?"

My libido began to hiss and a spell of lust fell around me, heat in my throat and knees, my eyes diving into the blue of hers, the heavy breasts pulling me toward her; her white neck softly turned and I wondered irrationally if her pussy was blond too, and I shuddered, ashamed, wondering, my God, what am I thinking at a time like this?

"Miss Quinlan," I groped. "Is that why my father ran away from the hospital?"

"It was the insulin injection. He wouldn't take it. Orinase — the kind you take in a pill — it didn't work on your father. He had to have the insulin by hypodermic, and it made him climb the walls, he hated it so."

I thanked her and asked her to get in touch with Dr. Maselli. "Tell him my father's at Angelo Musso's winery. Maselli knows all about it."

28

It was ten minutes down Highway 80 to the turnoff to Angelo's place, then half a mile up the hill to the winery. Circling the driveway at the rear of the house, I came upon Joe Zarlingo's Datsun camper. It didn't surprise me. (Later I learned that after telephoning Zarlingo from his hospital room that morning, my father had dressed and calmly walked out of the main hospital entrance, past the reception desk and out the front door, waiting on the hospital steps for Joe and his friends to whisk him away.)

The midday heat grabbed me by the neck as I stepped from the Chevy and crossed to a gathering of men under the grape arbor. The six were at the long picnic table, Angelo at one end, my father at the other.

Drooping majestically, my old man slumped deep in a wicker chair, wistfully drunk, his arms limp over the chair arms. He was like an ancient Roman patrician waiting for the blood to drain from his slitted wrists. Across from one another on benches were the four galoots from the Café Roma — Zarlingo, Cavallaro, Antrilli and Benedetti. They were all bombed but under control, swigging wine from thick tumblers. Jugs of Chianti and trays of food were spread over the long table: salami, sausages, prosciutto, bread and anise cakes. They had feasted long and well beneath the hot vine, and so had swarms of stunned bees, staggering over the food and floundering in puddles of wine, while hundreds droned mournfully among overripe muscats hanging from the vines.

Not a word was spoken as I came among them. It was as if I was of no importance, a nuisance, another bee. I moved quietly behind my father's chair and put my hands on his shoulders, his soft flesh drawing away, his bones so near to the touch.

"It's me, Papa."

He raised his head.

"What time is it?"

"Time for you to go back to the hospital."

"No, sir. Not me."

"You need your insulin."

He shook his head.

"Stop picking on your father," Zarlingo said. "Sit down, have a drink. Be quiet. Enjoy the party."

"I'm taking him back to the hospital."

"That's up to him." He reached out and touched my father's hand. "You wanna go back to the hospital, Nick?"

"No, Joe. It's nice here. Quiet."

The voiceless Angelo made a cackling sound, motioning me to come to his side, beguiling me with a toothless smile. As I moved toward him, he began to write something on a pad with a pencil, writing swiftly, slashing the paper, tearing off the sheet and handing it to me.

It was legible, but it was Italian.

"Can't read it," I said, handing it back.

Benedetti snatched it from my grasp. "Let me see it."

He studied the writing for a moment, then nodded approvingly at the old man. "Right," he said to Angelo. "You are always right, Angelo."

"What does it say?" I asked.

"It says, 'It is better to die of drink than to die of thirst.' "
I looked from him to the old winemaker.
"What's that supposed to mean?" I said, staring at Angelo's crumbling eyes. "I don't understand."
Quickly Angelo was writing again, another swift sentence, passing the sheet to Benedetti, who translated once more:
"It is better to die among friends than to die among doctors."
It brought applause, a clapping of hands, glasses held aloft and drained in a toast, even a wave from my father, who was beyond the point of understanding anything.
Encouraged, Angelo began to write once more. There was only one course left for me. I drew back my father's chair and tried to lift him, my arms around his chest. He fought me, feebly but in anger, squirming back into the chair. The paisani stared. They would not help me.
I said, "Please, someone, give me a hand. This man is very sick."
They sat there like tombstones. I began to cry. Not from grief, not anguish for my father, but compassion for myself. How good I was. What a loyal, beautiful son! See me trying to save my father's life. How proud I was of myself. What a decent human being I was!
I wept and pounded the table and the wine danced and spilled and the bees snarled. I tore my hair. I fell on my knees and clung to my father. "Come with me, Papa! You need care. You mustn't die in this wretched place."
His vague glance found me.
"Go home, kid. See what your mother wants."
I got up in shame and disgust and sat on the bench, sobbing. I had this talent for crying. It had brought me many rewards through my life, and some trouble too. When your weaknesses are your strengths, you cry. For crying disconcerts people, they don't know how to handle it; they are expecting violence and suddenly it vanishes in a pool of tears. I cried at my first communion. My tears broke Harriet down and she finally married me.

Without tears I could never have seduced a woman, and with them I never failed. It has laid waste the hearts of women who disliked me, and who wanted to kill me afterward for succumbing. I cried through melancholy passages of my own writing. The older I got, the more I wept.

Now Zarlingo was affected, reaching across the table to press my hand. "Take it easy, son," he soothed. "Wipe your eyes, have a drink. Don't worry about your father. He's strong as an ox."

I wiped my face and blew my nose. I forced down the wine. From the highway below came the wail of a siren, drawing closer, louder. I walked out to the driveway and saw a white ambulance streaking a trail of dust as it raced up Angelo's private road. As it slowed I saw two white-clad attendants in the cab. Dr. Maselli was with them. They leaped to the ground.

"Where is he?" the doctor asked.

He followed me into the arbor and moved to my father's side. Lifting the drooped head, he peeled back an eyelid. Removing a hypodermic from his kit, he filled it with a milky substance from a vial and injected it into my father's arm. Angelo and the other brothers gathered around, watching. They moved aside as the attendants came up with a stretcher. They carefully eased my father upon the stretcher and lifted him off the ground. As they carried him toward the ambulance each of his friends murmured farewell.

"*Ciao, Nicola. Buono fortuna.*"

"*Addio, amico mio.*"

"*Corragio, Nick.*"

"*Corragioso, Nicola.*"

My father lay motionless, eyes closed. Even the hot sun failed to disturb his eyelids. Now Angelo came to his side with a straw-wrapped bottle of Chianti and placed it lengthwise beneath his arm. It brought a frown from Dr. Maselli. The stretcher was lifted into the ambulance and the door closed. As the white car drove away my father's friends watched it churning dust toward the highway.

"He's gonna be all right," Zarlingo said.

"Sure he is," Cavallaro agreed. "He'll outlive us all."

"I'll drink to that," said Benedetti.

I got into the rented car and followed the ambulance.

For half an hour I waited on a bench in a hall outside the emergency room of the Auburn Hospital. When Dr. Maselli emerged, coatless, the look of death was upon him.

"He's gone."

"How, Doc? Why?"

"Cerebral hemorrhage. Swift, painless. A man couldn't ask for a better way to die."

As I turned to leave he asked, "Do you want me to tell your mother?"

"I'll tell her."

Down the hall in the pay station I telephoned Stella. She choked at the news and began to cry. We cried together for a long time, in each other's arms over the telephone.

I said, "Will you tell Mama?"

"Oh, God!" she sobbed. "Oh, God."

I hung up and walked out to the car in the parking lot. The waning day refused to cool and I was numb and unequal to the drive home to the agony of my mother and the empty space in the world now that my father was gone. Remembering the saloons along Chop Suey Street I thought of getting smashed, of losing myself in the semidarkness with those lonely old men peeling off their last days in one of those places.

As I started the car a nurse came down the hospital steps into the parking lot. It was Miss Quinlan. She was walking straight toward me carrying a white sweater, moving smoothly on low shoes, erect and clean and handsome, the sun behind her, piercing the space between her thighs. I stepped from the car and stood in her path. She paused and smiled.

"I'm sorry about your father," she said.

My eyes filled. I took her hands.

"Oh, Miss Quinlan, help me! I don't know what to do, where to go. What shall I do, Miss Quinlan? I'm lost. I'm wretched!"

She put her arm around me.

"There, there, Mr. Molise. I know how you must feel, I know. It takes time, my dear man. You must be strong, for your father's sake."

All my life was tumbling around me, and I seized upon her with my hands and with my grief. "Oh, please, Miss Quinlan. Fuck me, please, please. Save me, fuck me!"

She freed herself and looked straight into my eyes, startled, hesitant.

"You ask me to do *that?*"

"Oh, yes, Miss Quinlan! I love you, I adore you! Have pity on me."

She took a backward step and studied me.

"Well . . . it's possible, I guess."

"Please, dear, wonderful, beautiful Miss Quinlan!"

"I have to go to the supermarket first."

"May I come with you? I'll push your shopping cart."

"If you like," she smiled.

I smothered her hands with kisses and tears. I tried to fall on my knees but she held me up. "Don't do that, Mr. Molise. Stand up, please."

"Oh, thank you, angel. Thank you, thank you!"

We got in my car and drove to the market, my tears drying fast, Miss Quinlan at my side with her pretty nurse's hat over her blond Nordic braids, her knees like pomegranates under her hose, tight together, prim, so ladylike.

How delicious she looked, walking down the market aisles, selecting purchases, dropping them into the shopping cart. I insisted on buying her a bottle of Scotch and a coconut cake and thick lamb chops, and when we went through the checkout stand I paid for the whole damn thing, just to hear her gasp with gratitude and call me crazy. We got to my car again and I opened the door for her, and her magnificent derrière floated past my eyes like the grace of God, like the Holy Ghost. My old man would have loved it; he would have pinched it for sure.

We drove to her apartment, which was above a garage two blocks from the hospital. I carried the groceries while she unlocked the door. That apartment! It was like entering a hospital emergency room. All white it was, white tile along the sink, a white Formica top to the bar separating the kitchen and the living room, and still more white covering the stainless steel tubular chairs and divan. The sharp odor of Lysol cut across the atmosphere. Everything was closeted, hidden — dishes, pots and pans. Even the toaster on the bar was concealed under something plastic. At Miss Quinlan's instructions I put the sacks of groceries in the kitchen sink.

"You can undress here," she said crisply. "Put your clothes on the sofa."

She disappeared into the bedroom and locked the door. I pulled off my clothes and laid them out on the divan, neatly, in keeping with the austerity of the place.

As I finished, Miss Quinlan came from the bedroom. She was naked and not nearly as attractive as she had been in her nursing costume. Whereas I had conceived her a woman with spacious breasts, they were really almost nonexistent, sorry little dabs of flesh not much larger than a man's. Then I saw the flesh marks of falsies, which didn't disturb her in the least.

"Are we all undressed?" she said cheerfully, but with a professional intonation.

"Okay," I answered, standing up, hiding my precious loins with two hands.

She smiled.

"My goodness, aren't we modest." She gestured toward the bathroom. "This way, please."

I followed her into the bathroom, taking note of her drooping buttocks without the trimness her uniform created. The cleavage wasn't fetching either. Both buttocks just hung there lazily, carelessly, and I began to feel that Miss Quinlan was at least sixty.

I stood by as she filled the washbasin and stirred up a solution of soapsuds. None of this invigorated my sword, or, as my father called it, my *spada*. In fact, it began a sullen regression, and when Miss Quinlan grasped it there was little to seize, and she shook it and called it a shy and naughty boy.

"Prophylaxis!" she exclaimed, scooping soapsuds upon it. "That's the name of the game. Prophylaxis!"

The *spada* began to respond as she manipulated it with both hands. "The dear boy," she crooned. "He's such an angel." She handed me a towel, and as I dried myself Miss Quinlan made a soap and water solution, poured it into a douche bag, hung the bag on a hook, sat on the toilet, and plunged the douche nozzle between her thighs.

She toweled herself off, seized my *spada*, and marched me into the bedroom. By now I was without passion but overwhelmed with curiosity. Where would it all end? Miss Quinlan was a fiend but she was fun too, her flabby old buttocks bouncing as she pulled back the bedspread, kneaded the pillows, and nodded approvingly at the bed of love. On swift bare feet she dashed into the kitchen and returned with a jar of honey I had seen her purchase at the market.

"Jasmine honey!" she exclaimed, unscrewing the lid from the jar. "Taste!" She flecked a bit of it on her index finger and held it out. I opened my mouth to partake of it, but it wasn't for me at all, it was for my *spada*, a tiny dab with which to get acquainted, smack on the tip. With sudden and enormous energy the *spada* came forth, head aflame, and looked around, ready to fight. I felt a moment of shame. What a ghastly way to honor my poor father. But I was caught up in it, I had asked Miss Quinlan for it, and there was no reason to stop now, in spite of my father, my wife, and my two sons.

Seating herself on the edge of the bed, Miss Quinlan spread a thin layer of jasmine honey over my *spada*, from the scabbard to the tip. The golden gleam of it delighted her and with a murmur of desire she partook of the delicacy. The dear Miss Quinlan! She took everything — I felt it all going away and out of me, my sword, my glands, my heart, my lungs and my brains, a banquet for a rather elderly queen — and as the sorcery subsided she lay back on the bed, panting desperately, and I sat pooped in a chair. She had taken everything, and I had nothing to give in return.

And as she remained motionless, her arm covering her eyes, I moved to the bathroom and cleansed my sword with warm water and a washcloth. I saw her lying in the same position as I pulled on my clothes. My eyes scanned the apartment for a last look around. A cold, sterile place, but with a terrible beauty, the beauty of loneliness and two strangers sharing an intimacy, the beauty one felt but did not see. Unforgettable.

I started for the bedroom to say good-bye, but in the doorway I saw something that made me hesitate. Miss Quinlan lay as before, her arm shielding her eyes. But her hair had moved. That lovely pile of Nordic blondness wasn't real after all. It had slipped to the side, over her ear, revealing a white, bald skull. It humbled me. Had I stayed longer I would have burst into tears. How good she was!

"Thank you, Miss Quinlan," I said.

"You're welcome, I'm sure." It was a tired whisper.

She did not move.

"My father thanks you too."

"He was a dear man. I'm so glad I could help."

"Good-bye, Miss Quinlan."

"Good-bye."

29

THE DAY BEFORE the funeral Harriet arrived from Redondo Beach with our sons, and I was at the airport to meet them. She kissed me and stepped back to search my eyes for intimations of infidelity. She must have seen the death of my father in my tired gaze, and the strain of my grief, but I knew she didn't find anything of Miss Quinlan reflected there, for she gave me a trusting smile and kissed me again.

I had not seen my sons in a month. They had been in Ensenada on what they jestingly referred to as a fishing trip, having driven down there with two women in the van.

Dominic was twenty-four and Phillip two years younger. Their stubbled faces darkened by the Mexican sun, their hair down below their necks, they were dressed in denim jackets and pants, their feet in thonged sandals. They looked like rock freaks, not mourning grandsons of an old man gone from their lives.

Walking across the parking lot I said, "I hope you brought some decent clothes."

They looked at me in that cynical, aloof way of theirs, and Dominic said, "Don't worry about it, Dad."

"I don't want you at the funeral in those outfits."

"Yeah. We know."

"How about haircuts?"

"No way."

They tossed their grips into the luggage compartment and got into the back seat of the rented car. Harriet slid in beside me, and as I moved the car out I turned to her.

"Have they registered for the new term?"

"They said so," she answered doubtfully.

I looked over my shoulder at them.

"How about it, Phil. Did you register?" He was in Business Administration.

"Yes, Dad. All taken care of."

"How about you, Dominic?"

"I did not register," he said.

"Why not?"

"I took a job."

"What kind of a job?"

"I'm a checker in a supermarket."

"What the hell for? What about your degree?"

"I make seven dollars an hour. You know any marine biologists earning that kind of money?"

"Any jerk can check groceries. You need that degree."

"You didn't get yours," he said.

Harriet and I looked at one another in the usual bewilderment. We could not deal with them. They were spoiled rotten, those two, arrogant and sure of themselves. It wasn't their intelligence, it was their smug cleverness, their icy ability to verbalize. They never fumbled or groped for answers. They were omniscient and trigger-happy.

For a while we drove in silence. They lit small Mexican cigars and offered us the pack; Harriet took one but I declined.

"How old was Grandpa?" Phillip asked.

"In a few months he would have been seventy-seven."

''The old cock,'' Dominic smiled. ''He did all right.''

''What's that supposed to mean?''

''You know what I mean. You've told us a hundred stories about Grandpa.''

''I liked him,'' Phillip said. ''He used to take us to that old Italian saloon when we were little and show us off.''

''The Café Roma,'' Dominic remembered. ''He loved that vino.''

''And brandy,'' Phillip said. ''First thing in the morning, brandy in his coffee.''

''He had style,'' Dominic said.

We moved east on the freeway, the traffic light and swift. Clouds were piling up to the north and I wondered about rain at tomorrow's funeral.

''Dad,'' Phillip said. ''I have a question.''

''Fire away.''

''Are you a diabetic?''

I had thought much of it since my father's death, worried about it, discussed it with Dr. Maselli. Would it hit me someday? It was a possibility.

''No. I'm not a diabetic.''

''How about Dominic and me? It's inherited, isn't it? It's genetic.''

''The potential is there. Not the disease.''

''What's the difference?''

''Diet. Avoid sugar, and chances are it'll skip right over you.''

''Chances are it won't, too.''

''What are you asking for — a written guarantee? It's not a bad disease. You can live with it. Your grandfather proved that.''

''You're dreaming,'' Phillip said. ''There's no cure for diabetes.''

''No cure, but there's control, with insulin. Besides, you haven't got it, so what the fuck are you talking about?''

That chilled him and he was quiet, but Dominic came on: ''Dad, would you have had children if you'd known there was diabetes in your genes?"

I knew they were working their way to that question, and now that it was asked I found it hard to deal with.

"How should I know?" I said.

"No," Harriet said. "I wouldn't have had children."

Touché! The statement slammed the lid on a Pandora's box of silent speculation as the four of us pondered the nonexistence of Dominic and Phillip. Then the two began to laugh.

We drove to my mother's house and found it a place of doom and dirge, the cars of mourners parked on both sides of the street, my father's old friends slouched about the front porch drinking wine from Mama's treasured crystal glasses, vexed and uncomfortable from the wails of their wives inside. Italians loved their living, but sometimes they loved their dead even more, specially like these womenfolk gathered in every room of the house, swarming about my black-draped mother like dark ants around their queen, sobbing, rattling their rosaries, rolling their necks, embracing the distraught widow, pumping grief into her and intoxicated by the grief she pumped back.

I didn't blame Phillip and Dominic for not entering the house, and while they stayed in the car Harriet and I pushed our way up the porch and into Mama's bedroom where Harriet squirmed through the throng of sobbing women to my mother's side. She kissed Mama and came away with a sticky smear of tears across her cheek.

We could not remain there. Retreating to the kitchen, we saw the table heavy with salami, cheese, wine and fruit, preparations for hours of grief-venting, too much to endure, too absurd.

Slipping out the back way, we darted behind Mrs. Credenza's hedge next door and hurried along it to the street and the car. As I set the gears I heard Virgil's voice from the porch, frantically calling my name and running toward us.

"Have you seen Mario?" he asked.

"No."

''The son of a bitch. He was supposed to bring the pizza.''
I steered the car into the street and drove over to my mother-in-law's house. As Harriet and the boys got out I caught a glimpse of Hilda Dietrich peering from behind the curtained front door, and when I drove off she stepped out to greet them with open arms.

The end of my life in San Elmo was coming soon. After the funeral I would go away and never return, for without my father the town had vaporized into a wasteland of so many places like it. I knew what I must now do: take my mother away from there too, bring her under my own roof while Stella and my brothers worked out their own lives.

One other matter remained.

Like Paul, who had his moment of truth before Damascus, so too Henry Molise had had his fragment of ecstasy twenty-five years before in the San Elmo Public Library. I pulled up beside the graceful building, climbed the red sandstone steps my father had set with his own hands, entered the foyer, and strode down a corridor of bookshelves to that familiar place in the corner by the window near the pencil sharpener below the portrait of Mark Twain, and drew out the leather-bound copy of *The Brothers Karamazov*. I held it in my hands, I leafed the pages, I drew it tightly into my arms, my life, my joy, my sublime Dostoyevsky. I may have failed him in my deeds, but never in my devotion. My beloved Papa was gone, but Fyodor Mikhailovich would be with me to the end of my life.

30

I THOUGHT MY father's funeral would bring out the whole town, but I was mistaken. More people had attended the wake on the previous afternoon than were present at the church service. Most were members of the family, and many were grandchildren who didn't want to be there in the first place, for the circus was in town at the fairgrounds and the kids were annoyed at their grandfather for picking such a lousy time to die. The rest of the mourners were friends and neighbors of my mother and a loyal group from the Café Roma.

Waiting gloomily in their Sunday clothes, the pallbearers shaded themselves under a big elm on that hot, cheerless afternoon. They were Zarlingo, Cavallaro, Antrilli, Mascarini, Benedetti and Rocco Mangone. They were as beautiful as old stones strewn across a patch of hillside. Grief plucked at my throat like the leap of a trout as I looked at them. Now that I had none, I would have taken any one of them for a father. Indeed, any man, or bush, or tree, or stone, if he would have me for a son. I was myself a father. I didn't want the role. I wanted to go back to a time when I was small and my father stood strong and noisy in the house. To hell with fatherhood. I was never born to it. I was born to be a son.

The pallbearers doffed their hats as Harriet and I entered the church. I waved. I wanted to shout: "I love you, I need you, take care of me, you funny old men!"

The family was gathered in the two front pews before the main altar, my mother in the first pew between Virgil and Stella and their families. Mama wore a black veil covering her hair and face. Harriet and I and our sons slipped into the pew behind them, next to Peggy and her kids. Right away I noticed that one of us was missing. I turned to Peggy.

"Where's Mario?"

"In a state of shock. I told him to stay home."

Virgil glanced over his shoulder and sneered.

"With the Giants and Atlanta playing a doubleheader on TV? That's funny, Peggy. Very funny!"

"It's true!" Peggy hissed in a loud whisper. "He cried and cried. He really loved his father. But you were all against him. You alienated him. Why did you pick on him? Why didn't you have a little faith in him? Well, you'll see. You'll be sorry, all of you!"

"God help you, baby," Virgil smirked.

"You fucking bank clerk!" she raged. "You're not fit to clean Mario's shoes!"

"Says who?"

"Says me, you creep."

"Shh!" Mama chided under her black veil. "Please. Papa's dead."

Then the hearse arrived and the pallbearers carried the brown casket down the aisle to the communion rail. The mourners watched the attendants bring funeral wreaths and bouquets of flowers to place around the casket. How small the casket seemed. My father had been a bull of a man, but not tall. Horizontal in that box, he seemed no larger than a boy.

Then an enormous wreath was brought down the aisle, all

roses and carnations and ferns, so large that two attendants carried it. They placed it at the foot of the coffin and stood it up on wire brackets. It was six feet tall, a gaudy splendor, very impressive. It bore a strip of white silk upon which a red inscription was embossed. It read:

COMPLIMENTS OF CAFÉ ROMA.

The pallbearers gazed at their tribute with pleasure and satisfaction. No question about it, the Café Roma brotherhood had come through with the biggest and the best. My mother, bless her, was so impressed that she turned, raised her veil, and nodded in appreciation. The Roma boys smiled in sympathy.

A bell tinkled and Father Martin emerged from the sacristy behind two altar boys. Beneath the boys' cassocks you could see the green and white stripes of their baseball socks, and you knew that somewhere in the town their teammates were waiting for them.

Father Martin moved down to the casket, blessed it with holy water, and read the Latin rites from a missal. Closing it, he put his fingers together and tried to assemble his thoughts as people waited for him to speak. It must have been a problem, for he was dealing with the life and death of a man who had rarely come to church and who had never performed his Catholic obligations.

"Let us pray for the soul of Nicholas Molise," he began. "A good and simple man, an honest man, a fine craftsman who lived among us for so many years and gave his best for the improvement of the human community. Instead of weeping, let us rejoice that he has come to the end of his toil on this earth, and is now at peace in the arms of his Father in heaven."

That was it, short and sweet, a bull's-eye. The mourners joined him in the recitation of the Lord's Prayer, and he concluded with: "Eternal rest grant unto him, O Lord, and let the perpetual light shine upon him."

The padre returned to the sacristy as the undertakers opened the casket and my mother led the mourners past the body. She raised her veil and kissed her husband on the forehead. Then she laced her white rosary around his stiffened fingers. Virgil led her away as she cried softly. One by one we passed the bier and stared down at Papa, the children startled, horrified, fascinated, the others weeping silently.

I did not weep. I felt rage, disgust. Good God, what had they done to that poor old man! What had they done to that craggy, magnificent Abruzzian face, those lines of pain and toil, the resolute mouth, the cunning knit of his eyebrows, the furrows of triumph and defeat! Gone, gone . . . and in their place the smooth, unlined, cotton-stuffed face, the rouged cheeks. It was a shame, an obscenity, and I was stung with a writer's wickedness, thinking, that's not my old man, that's not old Nick, that's Groucho Marx, and the quicker we bury him the better.

31

TEN CARS of mourners followed the hearse across town to the cemetery a mile away, behind the high school gym. We had a police escort, a cop on a motorcycle leading us through the deserted little town, everybody having gone to the circus. No traffic at all, only the slow-moving funeral procession over the bridge to Pacific Street. My car followed the hearse, Mama sitting between Virgil and me.

"Didn't Papa look great?" Virgil said. "God, the things they can do nowadays."

"He looked happy," Mama said. "It's the way he used to be, always laughing, always making jokes."

The joke was on Papa, but I held my tongue.

At every intersection the cop brought his Harley to a halt, raised his arm, glanced to the left and the right, blew his whistle, and waved the hearse to proceed. It was twelve blocks to the graveyard and he stopped the procession at all twelve intersections. My mother watched, deeply impressed, her veil lifted, for the escort gave her husband an air of importance, as though he'd been a big man in the town.

We moved slowly through the cemetery gates and past the "new" graveyard to the "old" one, the difference being that the new section was without ornate tombstones or large trees, whereas the old place was a brooding fairyland of grotesque marble figures beneath enormous oaks and sycamores, luxuriantly shaded, the grass moist and very green and uncut, as if to devour the ancient sunken graves. Through the trees we could see Father Martin standing before an opening in the ground, waiting, prayer book in hand.

I helped my mother from the car and she choked back a cry as she moved toward the priest. As I started to follow, Virgil snatched my arm.

"Let's watch it now," he cautioned. "Keep her between us. She might try something."

"Try what?"

"Jumping on the coffin."

The thing was possible, but it didn't happen. Each of us held her by an elbow during the last rites, and though she swayed as she watched the casket descend, the pulleys squealing, she remained composed and without grief. Afterward Father Martin came to her side and took her hands in his and she looked up at him and began to cry. He bent and kissed her on the forehead and that made everybody cry, adults and children alike, and people turned away and tried to hide their misery as they drifted back to their cars.

Harriet joined me and we escorted Mama away through the sycamores. Then, from a distance, we heard it: a voice, mechanical, electronic, pulsing across the land and through the trees as if to make every leaf tremble, a cry of battle, growing louder. We stopped to listen. It was a radio voice, a sportscaster, tense, explosive, profaning the holy cemetery with alien vibrations.

"Bottom of the ninth!" the voice proclaimed. "Two out. Bonds at second, Rader at third, Kingman the batter. The count: two balls and two strikes. Capra in a full windup. Here's the pitch: a ball!"

Through the trees lurched Mario's battered truck, nuts and bolts jangling, the voice strident as it swept down upon us. Joy brightened my mother's face.

"It's Mario!" she exulted. "Oh, Mario! He came after all. I knew he would, I knew it! Oh, thanks be to God!"

The truck skidded around a curve and braked to a stop before us, throwing gravel. The radio's irreverent hysteria seemed to jeer at the peaceful dead, rude, flouting their eternal sleep.

Kingman had struck out. The Giants had lost. Momentarily Mario caved in upon the steering wheel. He snapped off the radio and returned to reality, looking at us.

"Am I too late?"

"No, Mario," Mama said. "There's still time. Hurry, before they cover him up!"

He jumped from the truck and walked quickly toward the grave where two men with shovels were preparing to fill the plot. We watched him look down upon the casket, covering his face with both hands as he began to cry. Then we walked to the car.

My mother got between Harriet and me. She took off her veil, leaned back and sighed. Her face was beautiful, her eyes were warm with a sense of peace. She took my hand.

"I'm so happy," she said.

"He died quickly," I said. "He didn't suffer at all."

She sighed.

"He worried me so, all the time, from the day we were married. I never knew where he was, what he was doing, or who he was with. He wouldn't tell me anything. Every night I wondered if he'd come home again. Now it's over. I don't have to worry anymore. I know where he is. That he's all right." She uttered a little moan. "Oh, God. The things I used to find in his pockets!"

I started the car.

"Let's go home."

"I bought a leg of lamb," she said. "We'll have a nice dinner. The whole family. With new potatoes."